PRAISE FO

M000308363

"*Prey No More is filled with terrific characters, both good and bad, and writing that moves a breakneck speed. Fabulous second installment of the new series, The Desire Card.*"

JEN CONLEY AUTHOR OF *CANNIBALS: STORIES FROM THE EDGE OF THE PINE BARRENS*

"*Gripping and relentless!*"

VINCENT HAUUY, BESTSELLING AUTHOR OF *LE TRICYCLE ROUGE* AND *LE BRASIER*

"*A twisted and cinematic new series stoked by greed.*"

LUKE JEROD KUMMER, AUTHOR OF *TAKERS MAD* AND *THE BLUE PERIOD*

# PREY NO MORE

## THE DESIRE CARD BOOK TWO

### LEE MATTHEW GOLDBERG

ROUGH
EDGES
PRESS

**Prey No More**
Paperback Edition
Copyright © 2022 Lee Matthew Goldberg

Rough Edges Press
An Imprint of Wolfpack Publishing
5130 S. Fort Apache Rd. 215-380
Las Vegas, NV 89148

roughedgespress.com

This book is a work of fiction. Any references to historical events, real people or real places are used fictitiously. Other names, characters, places and events are products of the author's imagination, and any resemblance to actual events, places or persons, living or dead, is entirely coincidental.

All rights reserved. No part of this book may be reproduced by any means without the prior written consent of the publisher, other than brief quotes for reviews.

Paperback ISBN 978-1-68549-091-1
eBook ISBN 978-1-68549-090-4

# PREY NO MORE

"Kill or be killed, eat or be eaten, was the law; and this mandate, down out of the depths of Time, he obeyed."

—**Jack London,** *The Call of the Wild*

## PART ONE

# ANY WISH FULFILLED FOR THE RIGHT PRICE

A BLIZZARD FALLING, PUNISHING FLAKES THE SIZE of dimes. The snow beginning to stick. A Vermont wilderness with mountains in the distance, and a tiny cottage perched on a hill, quaint and ominous at the same time. A light turns on in the bedroom, a pathway of illumination to this nighttime painting.

Inside the cottage, a man has entered the bedroom, the sole lamp proving how sparsely it's kept. Not a home but a place of rest. A bed in the center, the sheets tucked in military style. Nothing on the walls except for a postcard of Fiji with a declarative *Paradise!* written across the bluest sky ever. Sometimes the man stares at the postcard and dreams of a different life, but reality always jars him out of this fantasy. For he knows that paradise will only come when he's dead.

He carries a silver briefcase over to his dresser and begins to pack. A few documents. A plane ticket to Marrakesh. Photographs of a Moroccan man in his forties wearing a sharp white suit and ornate rings on each finger. He also tosses in a ratty copy of the novel

*The Call of the Wild* by Jack London and snaps the briefcase shut, its click the loudest sound he's heard all day.

He goes to the bed and pushes it a few feet over. Crouches down and feels for a groove in the floor. From under a floorboard, he retrieves a hefty stack of bills. He leaves the remaining cash. He puts the floorboard back and pats it down. Pushes the bed until the floorboard is covered. Walks over to the dresser and opens the top drawer.

Inside: a James Dean mask, the likeness unmistakable. Not a cheap mask bought at a costume shop. He puts it on and it fits the contours of his face perfectly. At a quick glance, it could almost look real.

He stares into the mirror and combs the hair attached to the mask as if it's his own. Styles it diligently to achieve an ideal coif, a slicked-back approximation of who he is now, this movie star forever eternal.

Once he takes off the mask, the likeness to James Dean is gone. Ordinary good looks stare back in the mirror, someone who can slip through crowds despite well-built arms and an imposing frame. Skin paler than most but not grossly pale, an indication of time spent traveling from shadow-to-shadow. Short black hair and thin lips that rarely ever smile. Nothing truly identifiable except for a nasty diagonal scar over his right eye, the cut so deep it reached bone, a mark that will always tie him to the past.

Both the cash and the James Dean mask are tossed in the briefcase. He takes a deep breath, one last gasp of Vermont's Zen-like chill before he switches to machine mode and heads to the airport.

———

On the plane, the passengers are all asleep but the man is alert, as always. Under a tiny light he studies various documents of the Moroccan gentleman with the ornate rings on his fingers. Name: Hasan Bouchtat, Status: Married with two children, CEO of Bouchtat Incorporated – a real estate conglomerate, Home Address: 310 Rue el Adarissa, Marrakesh.

On the man's tray table is a half drank glass of Scotch neat. He reaches into his pocket, takes out a vial of prescription pills, and pops two into the glass. Downs the rest in one gulp, his left eye fluttering from the sting.

He raises the window to his right, an orange sun winking across the horizon, the plane starting to dip as land materializes below.

IN THE OUTSKIRTS OF MARRAKESH, THE MAN drives down an empty two-lane road. Debussy glitters over the rental car's speakers, *Prelude A L'Apres Midi D'un Faune*, the swirl of notes putting him at ease. The silver briefcase sits in the passenger's seat. Monotonous scenery whips by, miles of dirt and rock formations, as if the world succumbed to an apocalypse. A GPS on the dashboard beeps as he checks the coordinates. He slows down to a crawl.

Dust attacks all sides of the car due to a passing gust of wind. From out of a beige cloud, an old man in a white *djellaba* emerges on the side of the road, his frail body barely filling out the cloak. In his gnarled hands, he holds an object wrapped in rags.

The man stops the car as the dust storm settles. He can still see the thick of it in the old man's teeth. The silver briefcase is opened and the stack of cash removed. He turns down Debussy and lowers the window.

"*Good morning*," the old man says in Arabic, his

voice sounding like sandpaper rubbing up against more sandpaper. *"Please state your I.D."*

"James Dean."

The old man gives a solitary nod. He passes over the object in rags and takes the money.

The man uncovers the rags to find a Walther PPK/E semi-automatic pistol with a silencer. Exposed hammer, traditional double-action trigger mechanism, single-column magazine, a fixed barrel and a blue steel finish.

*"This will do,"* he replies, his Arabic passable.

*"You have never met me before,"* the old man warns, in his native tongue. A shaking finger pokes through the open window. *"I am a ghost."*

The old man steps back from the side of the road. He flips a hood over his head, his face vanishing.

The man wraps the gun in rags and places it in his briefcase. He turns Debussy back on, louder than before, loud enough to cause the car to shake.

He speeds down the road until the old man is nothing more than a fading dot amidst the bleak landscape.

————

A posh hotel lobby in Ville Nouvelle. Charming and decorated in an old Moroccan style, muted turquoise and orange floral mosaics along the walls, a large pool banked by gardens in the back.

The man walks up to the front desk, silver briefcase in hand. The front desk girl is all smiles, her skin the color of dark honey.

"Hello, welcome to Marrakesh."

"Yes, hello."

He hands her his passport.

"J.D. Storm," she says, typing his name into the computer, her tongue lolling in her mouth as if it sounded wrong. Maybe it just seemed that way because he was so used to being called another name now.

"You're all set, Mr. Storm," she says, handing over his passport and giving an even perkier smile. "Are you here for business or for pleasure?"

He hasn't blinked yet during their entire conversation.

"Business."

———

In the hotel room, J.D. sits with the shades drawn. He's tapping his foot to the Debussy concerto. Finally, he stops and takes out a small earpiece from his briefcase. Fits it into his eardrum and presses until it lights up.

"Gable, please," he says. "It's Dean."

A crackling sound as he waits, his bowels rumbling.

"Location?" a voice finally asks. It sounds digitally altered, the tone deep and unnerving. A robot you do not want to mess with.

"I'm at the Es Saadi Palace in Marrakesh," he replies. "I've met with the courier."

"I trust it will be completed tonight?"

J.D. doesn't respond immediately, his first mistake. A drop of sweat trickles down his cheek.

"Yes, sir."

"That's my good soldier," Gable responds. "But you did just hesitate. I could hear it in your voice."

J.D. makes a fist. "No, it was the connection."

"I don't want a repeat of what happened in New York with the girl."

"I can assure you–"

"You hesitated then. This is an even tougher assignment."

"Yes. I know."

"Repeat our mantra for me. What does the Desire Card say?"

"We promise to fulfill any wish for the right price."

"And this wish is paying astronomically. So don't fuck it up. Check in with the main office once it's done."

Gable hangs up and J.D. removes the earpiece. He catches a glimpse of himself in the mirror. He doesn't want to think about New York, but New York comes pummeling through the door, reeking.

An alleyway off the West Side Highway. Club music pumping from down the street. Wearing his James Dean mask with Humphrey Bogart at his side. The Desire Card demanded that they embrace their other persona, to live and breathe as someone who once touched greatness, as opposed to the scavengers they truly were. Gable's collection of the morally bankrupt, the ethically unsound, the scraps of society who had no other choice but to comply. So they all signed in blood and are now just waiting for Hell to come knocking.

"Get the chloroform ready," Bogart had said, in a deep robotic tone just like Gable's. He checked his watch. "The club is about to close."

J.D. failed to move.

"What's the problem?"

"We've never gone after a woman before."

"You haven't gone after a woman, but I have. It is no different than anyone else."

"What's next? Children?"

The thump-thump of the club beats got louder. Bogart hadn't responded yet. J.D. couldn't tell what the guy was thinking. This was the first time that he ever vocalized how he felt to another operative. He barely allowed himself to think it before, as if Gable had the uncanny ability to tap into his mind.

But Bogart was a friend, as much of a friend as one could have at the Desire Card. They had been on missions together going on seven years with clients spanning across the globe: the Ukraine, Belgrade, even freezing in Antarctica as they zeroed in on their target, two snipers parallel to one another in a land of frozen snow. Bogart enjoyed classical music too, partial to Bach. J.D. remembered the guy passing over a headphone while they waited for their mark to emerge in the white abyss. *Orchestral Suite No. 3 in D* filled up the barren void, made J.D. feel warm inside despite any early stages of hypothermia. But he had never seen Bogart's real face. He had no idea who he truly was.

"It isn't right," he said to Bogart, in the alleyway.

"You keep telling yourself that when we're at the bottom of the East River if this job isn't finished."

"What did this girl do to deserve–?"

He knew he should shut up and pretend to be joking. The mantra of the Desire Card was all that mattered—*ANY wish fulfilled for the right price*, everything else meaningless.

"I'd stop asking questions now if you know what's good for you."

He wished he could tell if Bogart was trying to be

consoling, a friend letting him know that his wild thoughts would only bring trouble, not an adversary who'd be ready to slit his throat at the first sign of insubordination. Their voice boxes made it impossible to discern. And yet, he continued.

"Where do we draw the line?"

This was the question that often slipped into his thoughts during nights without enough substances to obliterate him into dreamland, when the cracks of the ceiling became the bane of his existence. Counting 1...2...3...4...and all-the-way-to-a hundred thousand. Till sun-up if that was what it took to get him there.

"There is no line," Bogart said, with a hint of sadness. But the guy wasn't sad. J.D. knew he was only imagining this, anything to make Bogart appear more human.

The club music down the street stopped. J.D. could hear his heartbeat getting louder.

*Thump. Thump. THUMP.*

"Where is the chloroform?" Bogart insisted.

"I...I..."

He could hear the sounds of heels clicking down the sidewalk.

Bogart peered out of the alleyway. "Forget you. I see her. I'll take care of it myself."

Bogart removed a heavy-duty police baton from his trench coat as a pretty Dominican girl in her twenties danced down the street, the music from the club still a part of her walk. Hoops on her ears, thick in all the right places, visibly inebriated. As she passed by the alleyway, he pulled her into the shadows.

Her screams were silenced by the sound of the baton thwacking against her skull.

J.D. SETS OUT IN THE BOILING AFTERNOON SUN, HIS rental car creeping towards 310 Rue el Adarissa. The Hivernage neighborhood chic and verdant. Grand hotels and casinos surround. Palm trees flank the streets, North Africa with a Floridian vibe. He slows as he reaches the address, a ritzy villa. He drives around the block until he's facing the backyard from across a roadway.

All is quiet on the street, no foot traffic.

Through a giant window he can see the movements of a Moroccan woman and two small children. She is wearing a lavender *kaftan* decorated with golden ornaments, definitely not the nanny.

He opens the silver briefcase. The pistol sits next to the James Dean mask, but he reaches for *The Call of the Wild* instead. He turns to the first page – Part I: INTO THE PRIMITIVE.

A photograph of a tough-looking elderly man wearing WWII fatigues slips out. Flipping it over, he reads a note written in cursive.

J.D.,

*Nothing in life will ever be easy for you. Parents in their graves before you could walk, a bedridden and penniless old fart like me raising you. You will be beaten time and time again, but never let it break you. This book's words kept me alive in Monte Cassino. Use it for inspiration when you're in the trenches and need it most.*

*-GRAMPS*

An image of Gramps coalesces, the old man insistent on wearing his uniform one last time fifteen years ago before cancer got him. J.D. snapping the picture for an obituary in the local *Newburgh News*. Gramps still sturdy, despite the shakes and losing thirty pounds over his last few months. Stars and medals on his chest. Proud of his history and optimistic of J.D.'s future once he turns eighteen. Soldiers running in their blood ever since the Storms migrated to America after the 1916 Easter Rising caused the family to seek a life outside of Ireland. A Depression Baby with dyed hair the color of scrambled eggs, slicked-back with Brylcreem, the product of a generation that no longer existed. Never a penny wasted, never a tear shed, still thinking the world was in an endless combat along with constant conspiracies of a World War III. Skim milk with an ice cube after every meal, sometimes a glass of harder stuff too. Their modest house smelling of pipe smoke, of blackened pans left on the burner, of a home without women. A basement full of rifles, and a young J.D. learning to shoot cans on the back porch before he graduated to weekends spent hunting. Crouching in the woods, Gramps nearby with a cigarette jammed in his sneer, a prancing buck in their sights. Gramps nodding as J.D. shut one eye and got the buck every time.

"A natural," Gramps would say, kneading J.D.'s shoulder, never smiling but certainly pleased. His wet cigarette handed over for a congratulatory drag.

"But they ain't all bucks," Gramps continued, rubbing the spot where a bullet once tore through his leg. "A goddamn *Kraut* got me from behind. You must always be looking over your shoulder, son, for evil won't announce it's coming. Say it with me again, 'Evil won't announce it's coming'."

J.D. would repeat that phrase every time; the words causing a chill to zigzag down his spine, even if they were hunting in a summer heat.

And even though he didn't listen to Gramps' advice years later when it mattered most, after that unfortunate lapse in judgment, he swore to never make the same mistake twice.

WHILE WAITING FOR THE MARK TO ARRIVE HOME, J.D. gets caught up in reading *The Call of the Wild*, imagining Gramps' gravely baritone narrating the prose. He flips a little further into the novel until he reaches a highlighted passage:

> *"Kill or be killed, eat or be eaten, was the law; and this mandate, down out of the depths of Time, he obeyed."*

The phrase like a knife, an absolute truth, how he had whispered it in the military plane before touching down in Kuwait and made sure to repeat it five times a day, as if it became his own version of a Muslim prayer. How he then had it tattooed on his arm years later after returning from that hellish job in New York City, its meaning forever changed.

He rolls up his sleeve now and runs a finger across the letters.

Outside the sun is about to set, a pink ball tucked behind the Atlas Mountains. Not quite the same scenery as Iraq, but close enough to shuttle him there. Every day something was bound to cause his mind to return, final puffs of his conscience unwilling to let go.

He continues tracing the quote with his index finger and is taken back to the counterinsurgency in Siniyah almost a decade ago. Hunting for Iraqis suspected of attacks on coalition forces. Three weeks out of the training course in Fort Benning, Georgia where he learned to stalk his prey, conceal his movements, spot telltale signs of an enemy shooter, and take down a target with a lone shot. All the other snipers were men just like him, none of them cocky grunts or jokesters, but quiet, unflappable marksmen with a dispassionate intensity. Their silence said enough.

Adrenaline was coursing through his veins that morning in Siniyah. The possibility of a first confirmed kill, even though none of his team ever bragged about their feats—for there was no pleasure in killing, only icy professionalism.

Perched above a possible insurgent's hideout, he lay splayed in the hot sand, a standard M24 S2S sniper rifle locked in his grip, his finger flirting with the trigger. This had been his baby for the last few weeks; carrying it in a padded green canvas bag, naming it Duluth after a girl he left behind who was already starting to feel like nothing more than a dream. Adjustable Kevlar stock, a thick stainless-steel barrel, mounted telescope, day and night scope, bolt action rather than semiautomatic. Firing 7.62 millimeter ammunition with the ability to hit a target from a thousand yards away. He waited for that target to appear, for his purpose in life to be revealed.

A sliver of pink sun flitted along the horizon, everything else shrouded in darkness. No sign of movement below. He rubbed his weary eyes and turned to Clinton, his spotter just a few yards away. Clinton's own eyes a spider web of bloodshot veins. This was day two of a sleepless mission that looked like it might drag on into day three. Hours bleeding into hours without any indication that the hideout was even occupied, but still they waited. Clinton with a wife and baby girl back home in Delaware, their pictures taped to the inside of his helmet, whatever it took to keep them in mind. J.D. avoided bringing any pictures, just *The Call of the Wild* as a mantra to help him return home.

Soon the pink sun fizzled and darkness reigned. The vision from his goggles bathed the world in a nuclear green. A wisp of gunfire rang out in the muted distance, no way to tell if it was friendly or not, just a spiral of smoke bringing life to the still scene. And then, Clinton pointed in the other direction. A beat-up car snaked through the road toward the hideout, the driver's side window covered with a sheet. J.D. removed the condom he had placed over the gun muzzle to keep the sand out. He followed the creeping car with his scope. No way to know if the driver was a threat, but Clinton gave the signal, and when your spotter, your brother, gives that signal, you must comply, for the two of you are forced to trust each other more than you have ever trusted someone before. So he fired a few rounds at the car, the bullets ripping through metal and coming out the other side. Clinton gave a thumbs up, and J.D. watched as the car rolled to a stop.

The driver had fallen against the horn, the sound piercing through the night.

And then, chaos took over.

# 5

BACK IN MARRAKESH, THE SOUND OF A CAR HORN echoes through the suburban enclave. J.D. shakes away the memory of Siniyah, realizing that he's been leaning on the car horn. He snaps back, looking around to see if anyone has noticed, but the streets are empty.

In the mark's house, he can see that the wife has changed into a nightgown and her children are in their pajamas ready for bed. They have moved to the front door. Someone is home.

He puts on the James Dean mask and grabs the pistol from his briefcase.

The mark steps inside, the same man from the pictures. Attractive olive complexion, polished white suit. His wife and kids greet him lovingly. A picture-perfect family J.D. is about to destroy.

The panic begins in his gut, bowels clenching, arms going numb, bugs crawling over his face. These attacks happening more frequently than ever before, this desire to run, to escape his mind. He pushes up the James

Dean mask so he can breathe. Counts 1...2...3...4...and all the way to a hundred thousand if need be. Luckily his breathing returns to a normal pace sooner than that, his heart no longer rattling in a cage.

"Get your shit together, soldier," he orders, and puts the James Dean mask back on.

When he looks at the villa again, the mark is nowhere to be found. The wife and kids have gone off to bed, the lights out. Finally, a light in the backyard snaps on.

The mark stands in the moonlight relishing a cigarette. The ornate rings on his fingers sparkling with each exhale.

J.D. slips out of the car with the pistol, silent as a ninja. He makes his way toward the backyard. Before the mark can finish his cigarette, J.D. is upon him. He clamps his hand over the guy's mouth, holds the pistol to the mark's temple.

"Do not make a sound."

The mark's eyes bulge. He tries to scream, but it is muffled.

"Be quiet and I'll leave your family alone. I'm going to remove my hand from your mouth now. Nod if you understand."

The mark nods, his face a mixture of tears and sweat.

J.D. slowly removes his hand.

"What are you?" the mark asks.

J.D. touches the James Dean mask with his free hand, as if he has forgotten he's wearing it.

"I am merely a messenger."

The mark presses down his wrinkled suit, glances up fearfully. "And what is this message?"

"A bullet between your eyes."

The mark begins to pray in Arabic, "*God is great, God is great.*"

J.D. pushes him to the ground. "I said be quiet."

"I have valuables. I am rich man." He shows J.D. the ornate rings on his fingers. "You can take whatever you want."

"I am not after your possessions—"

"Then why do you want to harm me?"

"Someone has wished for this, and I am here to fulfill that wish."

"Who?"

J.D. looks off into the night, as if it might hold the answer. "I don't know."

"Then why do you wish me dead too?"

"I don't have a choice."

"All men have a choice."

"Then I am no longer a man," J.D. says, aiming the pistol.

The mark has wet himself now, a trail of urine snaking down his trouser leg.

A glass door slides open and is slammed shut.

"*Father!*" a young boy cries in Arabic, no more than five, big doe-eyes. "*Father, who is this?*"

"Tell him to go back inside," J.D. orders.

"*Reda, go to sleep,*" the mark warns his son. The boy stands there mystified.

"Tell him to leave or there will be consequences."

"*Reda, this is a friend of mine. Go inside and I will be in soon.*"

The boy weeps, a dull ache from the pit of his stomach.

*"Reda, listen to your father. Please, it is past your bedtime."*

The boy lets out a wail and jumps into his father's arms, the two of them crying together.

The mark looks up, his eyes pleading. "I beg you, do not harm my son. Let me calm him down. You can kill me after."

Inside the house, a light turns on. J.D. can hear the wife stirring, her footsteps getting louder and louder against the hardwood floor.

"Goddamn, why did your kid have to come out?" J.D. says. His hand holding the gun has started to tremble.

"Please, you are better than this," the mark begs, a sniveling mess now. He rips off each shimmering ring, holding them out in the hopes that greed will consume this intruder. "Do not take my son's life. He...hasn't had a chance...to really live yet. He...he is just...just a little boy. Please...."

J.D. almost loses his grip on the pistol. He knows there are only two possible outcomes: kill the entire family or go on the run. Either way someone's dying.

"I can see that you are better than this," the mark says again, a final bid. He embraces his son tight enough to choke the boy.

Time freezes as J.D. watches this father embracing his boy, the bond between them overwhelming, *the need for one another to survive.* His arm holding the gun begins to lower. He engages the safety.

"No," he says. "That is not what you see when you look at me. What you see is someone who's now marked for death."

The wife's shrill voice bleats from an open window. A cry in the night as the suburban block awakens.

J.D. takes off across the lawn, the rental in his blurry sights. Once inside, he throws off the mask like it's made of poison and gulps incessantly in an attempt to catch his breath. He guns the gas and floors it, a tire streak left on the road as evidence of his hasty flight.

THE ES SAADI PALACE IS FULL OF FOREIGN travelers when J.D. returns, any one of them possibly working for the Desire Card, any one of them sent to take him out. Gable wouldn't take kindly to an unfinished job, often sending out his operatives to watch each other and eliminate any insubordination. J.D. would have no choice but to disappear.

He walks up to the front desk with the briefcase under his arm, a new girl there to greet him.

"Hello, sir, can I help you?"

An oozing line of sweat drips down his brow.

"Check out. I need to check out immediately."

"Last name?"

"Dean...I mean...Storm. My last name is Storm."

She begins typing his info into the computer. "Storm...? Oh yes, someone just left a package for you."

"A package? When?"

"A few minutes ago, you must have just missed them."

"What did they look like?"

"I just started my shift. It was given to the previous clerk. One moment."

The girl leaves the desk.

J.D. looks over his shoulder and takes in each and every person in the lobby: a businesswoman, blond hair in a bun, mid-fifties, talking on her cell but she's glancing his way, just for a moment, before she walks off. He assesses that she's not a threat. But what about the stocky man, Middle Eastern descent with a thin mustache like some black and white movie villain? His nose in a newspaper and who the hell reads newspapers anymore?

The front desk girl returns with a medium-sized box. "Here you are, Mr. Storm."

He stares at the box, not wanting to take it.

"Mr. Storm? Are you all right?"

Finally, he tucks the box under his arm and heads to the elevator. He passes by the Middle Eastern man with a thin mustache who looks up from his newspaper just as the elevator doors close.

———

Pistol in hand, J.D. enters his hotel room. Immediately he goes to the window to see if anyone's watching and shuts the curtains. He checks the bathroom, the closet, under the bed.

All seems clear.

In the darkness, he places the box on the bed. Rubs his chin nervously before picking it back up and listening to it, making sure it's not a bomb.

No sound.

He lightly shakes it. Objects rattle around. He takes

a deep breath and opens it to find ten chopped off fingers, each cut below the knuckle, all with ornate rings.

"The fuck...?"

The box slips from his hands. The mutilated fingers beginning to swirl around.

He slaps his cheek to get it together. Grabs the box, parts the curtains and opens the window, tossing it into the alleyway below. The bloody fingers scatter amongst the garbage bins. Then he wraps the gun in rags and chucks it into the alleyway too.

————

As J.D. leaves the Es Saadi Palace with his silver briefcase, he knows he needs to be inconspicuous, but he's exploding on the inside, too freaked out to breathe. He hails a cab and jumps in, looking out the back window for a sign of anything suspicious. The business-woman with a bun has stepped outside as well. She's waiting by the curb on her phone, angry with whomever she's talking to.

"Airport," J.D. tells the driver.

The guy slowly puts the car in drive and creeps out of the parking spot.

"Faster," J.D. orders, and then he continues in Arabic. *"As fast as you can."* He opens the briefcase and throws a stack of bills into the front seat.

The driver's eyes perk up and he guns it.

As the taxi zooms away, J.D. swivels around to look out of the back window again. The businesswoman has gone, no trace she was ever there.

In Vermont, J.D. has only two things on his mind: get all of the cash that he's saved up over the years and get far, far away. He's surprised that Gable hadn't planted a syringe filled with strychnine on his seat during the plane ride, the Boss's favorite way of elimination. No telling if Gable already had operatives at the train stations, the bus depots. More likely he'd have to contend with a sniper perched in the snow-capped mountains, waiting for him to come home and turn on his bedroom light.

Long ago when he first joined the Card, he'd been sent to take out a rogue operative—a William Holden, who was pilfering clients for his own copycat company. A girl on retainer had been used as bait. She lured Holden into a dingy Motel 6 room in Hazlet, New Jersey, as J.D. stood behind a stained curtain. She began sucking off Holden when J.D. made his move, a bullet in Holden's brain. Brando and Astaire were outside with a garbage bin, a bag full of saws, and a ton of lye to dispose of the body. Somehow J.D. had justified that one, since Holden deserved his fate for crossing the organization. And Gable paid handsomely for J.D.'s allegiance; he was bumped up from trainee to operative after that swift kill. He had also found it easy to kill a guy whose eyes you couldn't see, who'd been nothing more than a mask representing someone who was already dead.

Now he rushes through mounds of snow to the cottage with his briefcase, tracking any possible movement or sound in the distance. An owl hoots and flaps overhead. He hears a crunch of snow to his right, but he can't see out of his periphery. Finally, a deer emerges from the darkness and scampers away.

He enters his cottage and shuts the door, a gust of winter wind following him inside. He locks every single lock. The whole house creaks with each step. He leaves the briefcase on the table and heads into the kitchen. In the back of a cupboard, he reaches for a large flour jar. Inside is a small 9mm semi-automatic. He goes to his bedroom and pushes his bed over a few feet. He removes the floorboards, but to his surprise nothing is there. The stacks of cash he once had are all gone.

"They've already been here," he whispers.

*Or they still are.*

He hears a sound outside, another crunch in the snow. This time there is no deer scampering away.

A shot blasts through the window and grazes his ear. Blood drips to the floor.

He ducks down and glances outside.

The silhouette of a man is running toward the cottage.

Keeping low, he crab-walks out of the bedroom

clutching his bloody ear and then makes a break for the front door.

A shot rings out again as the locks are blasted off. The front door bursts open.

A man wearing a Humphrey Bogart mask stands there with an SR25 sniper rifle. He goes to hit J.D. with the butt, but J.D. ducks and charges at him, knocking Bogart to the floor. The SR25 spins across the room.

Bogart forces the 9mm out of J.D.'s hand. With his hands free, J.D. rams Bogart's head into the floor. Bogart is stunned for a moment, but then reaches up and sticks his thumb into J.D.'s right eye. J.D. doesn't scream as Bogart wedges his thumb into the socket. Deeper and deeper he presses, but still J.D. doesn't make a sound. A mystified Bogart finally sticks his thumb all the way in, causing J.D.'s eye to pop out of its socket.

The eye crashes to the floor, shattering into pieces.

Bogart is caught off guard. J.D. uses the opportunity to grab the 9mm back and stick it in Bogart's face.

"Talk!" he says, as both men try to catch their breath.

"What just happened?" Bogart asks, his robotic voice quivering. He stares at the shattered eye.

"Did Gable order this?"

He frisks Bogart for any concealed weapons, finds none.

"How can you be such a good marksman with one eye?" Bogart asks. He reaches out to pick up a piece of glass pupil.

J.D. points the 9mm in Bogart's nose. "I'll show you how a good a marksman I still am. Now talk!"

"What can I say that you haven't already figured out?"

J.D. clobbers Bogart's forehead with the 9mm's handle, causing a dent to form in the mask.

"How many of you are waiting outside the cottage?"

Bogart gulps for air, a robotic wheeze. "It's just me."

J.D. looks into Bogart's eyes. There's no sign of life because of the mask. He cannot tell if Bogart is being truthful, or if they are about to be showered with other operatives blasting inside.

"You've put the organization in a very compromising position, Dean."

"The mark's kid was right there," J.D. says, softly. "How could I...?"

"Because it's your job!"

"What if I just walked away?"

He knows this request is futile, but still he tries to convince, to find a pebble of humanity in the avalanche their lives have become.

"You could tell Gable that I'll disappear. It would be as if I never existed."

Bogart lets out a mechanical laugh.

"You know too much. It would be sloppy to let you live."

J.D. grabs Bogart's collar in his fist. "I could say the same about you."

"I am not the only operative that will be sent. Like the myth of the Hydra, you cut off my head and two more will appear."

"Give me my money back and I'll let you live."

"Jimmy Stewart took all of your savings. Plus the extra amount you stored in your spot in the woods. He is long gone by now."

"How did you all know about my hiding spots?"

"The organization knows everything. Haven't you realized that by now?"

J.D. looks around the cottage, searching for any type of spy cameras.

"They are watching this unfold as we speak," Bogart says.

J.D. glances up at the ceiling, a faint whir rumbling from behind a light fixture.

"Fuck you," he says, pointing at the light fixture. "Do you hear me? Fuck all of this."

"Be resigned to your fate, Dean. There is nowhere for you to run."

"I'll find somewhere."

"You have no money. We are monitoring all the airports. I'm shocked you were able to slip past Cary Grant on your flight in."

"There aren't enough operatives to monitor every airport."

"As you know, the organization extends beyond just men in masks. We employ a network of part-timers that might look like your flight attendant, the pilot, or even a regular businesswoman on her cell."

He thinks back to the businesswoman on the phone in Marrakesh. She was probably there to deliver the package of severed fingers.

"The Card knows every place you've ever lived in so there is no point hiding out with friends or family," Bogart says, letting out a cough. "They will be killed too."

"I considered you a friend once."

Bogart shrugs his shoulders. *C'est la vie.*

"There are no friends in this business," Bogart says.

"Exactly."

An outside entity takes control of J.D.'s brain, the same one who visited him during that counterinsurgency in Iraq and throughout his early years at the organization, the same one with the ability to zap any last shred of morality.

He fires a slug into Bogart's stomach.

Bogart clutches the wound as blood pumps out, traveling in lines across the floor. He's struggling, blood spurting out of the mouth of his mask, thick like syrup, but J.D. manages to hold him down. Soon Bogart lets out a final gasp and dies.

J.D.'s lips are trembling. He sees the snow pouring into the cottage through the open door. He heads over to his briefcase on the table, takes out the James Dean mask, and holds it up to the ceiling.

"Can you hear me? Can you see what I've done? I'll kill whoever else you send after me. That is a promise."

He tosses the James Dean mask into the bloody puddle on the floor. He goes over to a bureau, opens a drawer, and removes an eye patch and a scarf along with a backpack. He dumps the contents of the briefcase into the backpack along with a tiny bit of cash from the back of the drawer.

He puts the eye patch over his right eye socket and ties the scarf around his head to stop his ear from bleeding. He grabs a coat and slings the backpack over his shoulder, then surveys the scene for one last moment before lugging Bogart's body out of the cottage.

———

With the 9mm in one hand, J.D drags Bogart through the snow leaving behind a nasty bloody streak as a pathway to the door. Once he's gone far enough, he lets go of the body as the snow dumps down on them. He climbs on top of Bogart.

"I wouldn't have gone after you. Even if Gable ordered it."

He begins to shake Bogart's limp body.

"You made me do this. You made me kill you!"

Bogart's mask flies off, his face full of deep scars that have healed but are still visible.

J.D. traces a finger down a scar shaped like a question mark that extends from Bogart's forehead all the way down to his lips.

"Why am I not surprised that you've been mutilated as well?"

He clutches the 9mm and takes off into the night, the snowfall building and building until it buries Bogart's body completely.

# 8

A FROZEN J.D. HITCHHIKES ALONG THE HIGHWAY, his face chapped, his extended thumb red and raw. The dark road is void of any movement; every sound an invitation that death could be lurking, waiting to strike. His mangled ear has gone numb, but blood no longer leaks from the scarf tied around his head, the wound a block of scarlet ice.

An occasional truck barrels by but never stops. As each pair of headlights floods the highway, he feels a twinge in his gut. Every truck could be a possible salvation, or just two tons of doom with an easy target in its sights. If Bogart was to be believed, the Card had other operatives in the area, all with the ability to commandeer a ride as a weapon since their sniper failed.

A twig snaps in the distance. His left eye peers around: just endless night and more night. He removes the 9mm from his backpack, his hand trembling, the gun trained on the dark expanse for any sign of movement.

Finally: sharp lights down the highway. He blinks

from their scrutiny. He takes a chance by putting the gun in his backpack so he could hold out his thumb again, praying that there is someone good left in this world.

Another twig snaps, this time sounding farther away than before.

The truck slows to a stop, the engines sighing.

A burly guy in his sixties lowers the window. He has graying scruff with a chubby face like a bear cub and a gap in his front teeth big enough to fit a Chiclet. He's wearing a flannel jacket with a Carolina Panthers cap covering his eyes and a cross around his neck.

"Damn near run you over," he says. "It's darker than fuck out here."

"Almost wish you did," J.D. says, his teeth chattering so hard he's afraid they'll shatter. He readjusts the scarf around his wound as it begins to slip.

"That's a nasty cut you got there."

J.D. assesses this stranger, very carefully. Rabbit's foot dangling from the rearview, faded picture of a young girl with pigtails on the dash—possibly his kid. Doesn't appear to be threatening, but maybe the guy's just a little too perfectly homespun. He thinks back to the businesswoman in Marrakesh and that the Card often chooses to employ unassuming civilians as part-timers, those you'd never imagine would have a knife up their sleeve.

But if the trucker wanted to kill him, he'd already be long past dead.

"I said that's a nasty cut you got there, son."

"Took a tumble down a hill."

The trucker nods at this. Whether he believes it or not is another story.

"Where you looking to go?"

"Far from here. That where you headed?"

"Oh yeah, drivin' all the way to Seattle. That's my run. Takes about two days."

He'd been to Washington State a long time ago. Before the Card got him in their clutches. When he was still whole, and pure, and human.

"Yeah, I'd appreciate the lift."

"Looks like you would."

The door to the truck opens, a beacon of hope, the inside light warm, wonderfully smothering. He jumps inside, shuts the door, and holds his shivering hands in front of the heater.

"Not a night to be hitching. Colder than an Eskimo lady's tit."

J.D. manages the tiniest smirk but it fades fast. He can't even recall the last time he's heard something that's made him smile.

"Bud here," the trucker says, using his tongue to flick around some dip packed in the bottom of his lip. He extends his hand, but J.D. isn't done with the heater yet.

"We can shake later," Bud laughs, as he puts the truck in drive and continues down the highway. "Son, if you don't mind me saying but you look a right mess."

J.D. can move his fingers again, each digit gloriously crackling as it's brought to life.

"I've had better days."

"I sure hope so. Care to share? Usually got no one to talk to along my runs so I'd be happy to listen."

He knows he doesn't need a therapist, just a ride, but it's been a long time since he's had a normal conversation with someone: swapping stories, sharing pasts, the pleasure of being ordinary.

"Just couldn't stay here in Vermont."

"Well, how you know Washington's gonna be any better?"

"Cause it's not here."

Bud glances at the picture of the little girl on his dashboard.

"What about friends, family?"

J.D. shakes his head and watches the snow falling outside. It's coming down so hard that nothing else is visible.

"I had a girl up in Washington once."

"Oh yeah? How long ago did she strike your fancy?"

He allows himself to remember. It's a pleasant memory, one of the last good ones before his brain became rife with shit and more shit.

"About eight years, right before I shipped off to Iraq."

"Should've known you were a soldier. Got that quiet, serious kind of aura 'bout you. Nam here. Tour ended in '73. Man, I was young and dumb then."

"I never really got the chance to be young and dumb."

"So this girl, still sweet on her?"

"That was a different life."

"Where in Washington did she live?"

He tells himself to trust Bud because he has no other choice, because there is no one else. Fate sometimes places people in your life, for good and for bad, and he believes that wholeheartedly. There's a glimmer of Gramps in this guy's wink, in the lopsided smile that could be mistaken for a sneer. He's always looking for a glimmer of Gramps in everyone.

"She's in Killenroy. You know it?"

"I can certainly find it. Son, if I was younger and had a pretty blond girl waitin', nothing would keep me from that."

J.D. leans his head against the side window. Fatigue has started to set in.

"Would you mind if I close my eyes, Gramps?"

"I'll say nothin' more," Bud nods. "But I gotta wake you come dawn and move you to the back. Can't have no one seeing me with a passenger up front. Could lose my license."

"Thank you," J.D. says, his left eye tearing up.

"Think nothin' of it. If I hadn't driven by, you might've been dead before the snow melts."

"I still might be."

Sleep begins to consume him, drawing him out of reality, the snow a hazy reminder of what he's running from, his dreams a refuge from being hunted, of sun-drenched times when life seemed limitless, and of a beautiful blond girl stepping into a dive bar in a small logging town a week before he had to begin training at Fort Benning, hair past her shoulders, a dot of red on her lips, a sultry sway to her walk so all the boys would want to swivel their stools around; but she only smiles at J.D., so he orders her a Makers Mark because that's what he believes a girl like her would drink, and she does, hungrily, one after another until they're swapping dirty jokes in each other's arms and laughing hard enough to cry sweet tears.

*Take me back to her*, he whispers.

And in a blink, he's there.

9

EONS AGO, J.D. WAS JUST TWENTY-ONE YEARS OLD, a high school dropout with a resume that only said, *crackshot*. He'd never left New York State before, never had a legit job, burned up the little money left to him and was about to face foreclosure on Gramps' house. Even though he'd been in enough of a fog to miss out on the rah-rah 9/11 vengeance like all the other wannabe soldiers his age who'd already enlisted, he found himself a bit sober and heard about a baddie named Saddam and those Weapons of Mass Destruction. So he toyed with the idea of finally joining up. No girl, a few friends, a Border Collie named Gunner that recently went to dog heaven. He needed something other than cans to shoot at anyway. Then one night he had a black and white dream where a guardian angel dressed like an old movie star told him he was destined for greater things, nodded at his itchy trigger finger and swore that God gave everyone one specialty—that wasting his gift would be criminal.

So J.D. signed up the very next morning and saluted his new life.

After excelling in BCT (Basic Combat Training) and AIT (Advanced Individual Training), he had a week to kill before heading to Fort Benning so he scraped all the cash he had left for an epic road trip that would begin on the West Coast and trickle all the way down to Georgia. Washington seemed like the farthest point from Georgia he could think of so he closed his eyes with a map of the state and pointed to Killenroy, a hair away from the Canadian border. Boozing and messing around with tons of girls would be his agenda. Since he might return from Iraq as a ghost, he wanted a lay from every possible region.

At least that was his plan before he saw Annie.

———

The bar he wandered into where he met Annie had a neon gun firing the words Trigger Happy above the entrance. Not many other places to drink in a half-a-horse kind of town like Killenroy, but J.D. liked it that way. Cities caused his knees to knock together, country towns made him sing. It was late afternoon and the locals were already melting into their bar stools: tough biker types with beards, beady eyes focused on their fifth drink of the day. The hum of a country song on the juke. A lone stool at the end waiting for him.

This was back when he pounded drinks for fun, a cheerful drunk as opposed to using alcohol to dull everything. Trying shots with names that sounded like wild sex positions. And then, the front door swung open and in walked a dream.

Each tough guy spun their stool around. She had the face of a little girl who'd grown up too fast: high cheekbones that could stop any model scout, ruby red lips, and the tiniest button of a nose.

She sauntered past the row of derelicts that whistled and toasted her entrance. She didn't stick up her nose, this prettiest-girl-from-a half-a-horse-town. She basked in their infatuations and gave them all a sashay, but only saved a smile for J.D.

He shook away his buzz, blinked in awe. The regular sitting next to him got up in a drunken stupor to use the bathroom and this girl took the empty stool. The bartender hustled over to flirt, but before she could order a drink, J.D. piped up first.

"Two shots of Makers Mark," he said, because that's what he imagined she drank.

She gave no sign that she accepted his offer.

The bartender poured the drinks anyway. In a flash, she knocked back both shots and slammed each glass on the counter.

"Well, aren't you gonna order any for yourself?" she said, with a slow wink.

———

Annie Duluth from Coldstream, Kentucky, thick Southern twang like she was scooping each word out of her mouth, religious family with a wild daughter who wanted none of their fervor. Spun a globe when she was seventeen and landed on Killenroy just like him, hustled her way here the very next day. She smelled like lemons, and young J.D. thought he might be in love, something he'd seen happen in movies but never experienced firsthand before. She would become more than just a drunken lay, even though his brain felt pickled at the time. He imagined them getting married after he returned from Iraq, a bun in her oven that he'd name Jr., teaching the kid to shoot cans in the backyard like Gramps had done, and Annie waiting inside the house with a freshly baked pie and the warmest kiss on the planet.

"Wow...I-raq," she said, spacing out the word after he told her about his future. "I've never been nowhere but here and where I'm from."

"Me too," he said, with the toothiest grin ever.

"You have real pretty eyes," she said. "Blue like the sky. Well, not the sky in Killenroy cause it's always kind of grey here, but blue like a sky should be."

"You have a real pretty mouth," he said, because he was drunk and it was the first thing that came to mind.

She smiled again and it made her mouth look even prettier.

"My Momma always said that God places people in your life that you're supposed to meet. I don't believe in God, but I think I believe in that."

"I think I do, too."

He placed his hand on her knee and she didn't flinch, her skin smooth.

"I'm drunk as a fish," she said, in his ear. "Wanna hear a joke?"

He took in a whiff of lemon, nodded against her cheek.

"Man walks into a bar and the barman notices he's got a steering wheel stuck down the front of his trousers. 'Hey,' says the barman. 'What's that steering wheel doin' down your trousers?' 'Oh, don't start me on that,' says the man. 'It's driving me nuts!'"

She grabbed his balls, kneading each one. "Your turn."

"Okay," he said, pausing for a moment till one came to mind. "A guy walks into a bar in Iraq and asks the barkeep, 'How come there are no Walmarts?' The bartender responds, 'because there's a *Target* on every corner.'"

J.D. snorted through his nostrils, the Makers bubbling up his nasal cavity. Annie didn't make a peep. He wondered if he had offended her and wished he would've kept it light, but his head was swimming too much to censor. Iraq was creeping into his thoughts and there was no way to stop its thrust.

"Are you scared?" her beautiful mouth asked.

He shook his head. "I'm not scared of anything."

"That's cause you haven't really met me yet."

She kissed him on the mouth, hard enough for their teeth to clash, for his lip to bleed. She pulled away as red string of saliva still connected them. A burst of laughter erupted from their bellies, wild and untamed, as they folded into one other, lost track of place and time until he awoke from his stupor, threw some change on the bar, and spun her off the stool. They dashed into the dusk, barely able to keep their clothes on, naked by the time they reached his motel room, screwing all through the night and into the next day, stopping only to eat and use the bathroom until the week bled into a fog of that motel bed, and the sweat-soaked sheets that the maid grumpily cleaned each morning.

# 10

On their last night together, J.D. didn't want to have sex with Annie, he just wanted to hold her close so she could tell him that Iraq would eventually feel like a restless dream once he returned home. But Annie was in a primal mood.

"Please look at me," he said, tilting up her head. She responded by bucking against him even harder. "Annie–"

He tilted her head too fast, knocking it into his chin. He pulled away, using the sheets to catch the dot of blood from his bitten tongue.

"I'm sorry." She retreated to the other end of the bed.

"It's okay," he said. "It's just a nick. Besides, how about we just cuddle?"

He scooped her up, spooning her from behind. Her nose whistled at the end of each breath that he found too damn cute.

"You come from a big family?" he asked.

"Hmmm?"

"Sometimes I think about that. A farm somewhere with enough kids for a baseball team, and me, their old pop, teaching them how to hit a ball far enough to get lost in the sky."

"J.D.–"

"You ever think about being a mom? I bet you'd make a great one."

He crawled on top of her for a kiss, but she turned on her side. His lips grazed the fine peach fuzz on her jaw.

"What's wrong?"

"Nothing's wrong. I'm just fucked up so leave it at that."

She glanced at the clock on the nightstand and flung herself off the bed. A pool of their clothes lay tangled on the floor. She began separating hers to one side with her big toe.

"So, I gotta go," she mumbled.

"Gotta go where?"

He made an attempt to grab her arm, but she squirmed out of his grip.

"Are you mad at me, Annie? Did I do something?"

"I'm just wakin' up to reality, that's all. This week of dreaming has been great but–"

"I know I'm off to Iraq, but I want to stay in touch. We could write to each other, send pictures. Just hearing from you over there may be the only thing keeping me sane."

She wiggled into a pair of jeans and threw on a bra that had been dangling over a lampshade.

"That's sweet," she said, sighing. "You're sweet, real sweet, but I'm not. You need some good girl who'll wait at home for you and bake apple pies."

"That's not the only thing I want."

"You don't want me, I promise you. The kind of people I hang around with here, the ways I make a buck. I ain't fit for a soldier."

"I don't care how you make a living–"

"A living," she laughed. "Is that what I'm doing? Nah, I'm just buying time. I lie, I steal, I cheat...even some things worse than that."

"Like what?"

"Let's pretend I haven't said nothin'. You're off to defend America and don't need anything rotten getting in your way."

She tossed on a sweater and grabbed her purse.

"So this is good-bye?" he asked, his voice raising a few octaves. "Just like that?"

She scooped up one of the motel keys.

"Go to sleep and I'll stop by in the morning for a good-bye kiss."

"Let me come with you tonight. Where could you possibly need to go at one in the morning? It's not safe–"

She spun around, the key in her fist like a weapon.

"There's a liquor store a few towns over. Guys I know been staking it out. They gonna rob it and need a pretty girl to flirt with the guy behind the counter. Throw him off his game before they burst in with guns."

He didn't respond.

"Got nothin' to say, J.D.? Still want a picture from me now?"

"Who are these guys with guns?"

"Local trouble. I ain't sleeping with any of them if that's what you're thinkin'. Purely a business relationship."

J.D. pictured the tough bikers at Trigger Happy sitting on the row of stools. Names like Zedd, and Rat, and Crazy Town.

"I didn't think you were sleeping with them."

Tears crinkled at the corners of her eyes, her face flushed and red.

"You were the first guy I'd been with since–"

"Since what?"

She took a deep breath. "Since my ex beat the crap outta me and stole anything I had that wasn't pinned down. So I need to do what I can to get back on my feet, okay?"

"I'm not judging."

He spread out his arms and motioned for her to come close.

"You're not coming back in the morning for a kiss, are you?"

"J.D.–"

She wiped a tear from her cheek, chewed on her lip.

"I'll take it now, Annie, it's okay."

"My make-up's all runny..."

"You look beautiful."

He wrapped his arms around her and she put her chin on his shoulder. She was shivering like she was cold. When they kissed, it was like kissing a cadaver, there was no warmth to her anymore.

"Don't you die out there," she said, not looking him in the eye, already heading for the door.

He caught a glimpse of her blond hair bobbing away before the door shut and she was gone for good. He stayed up all night waiting, hoping each beam of light passing through the window might be her, longing for a real kiss that he could remember when he'd be deep down in the trenches.

Morning came with a bruised sun trickling through the blinds, but Annie never returned. He balled up the soaked sheets they spent all week in and chucked them in his duffel before hitching all the way down to Georgia, a lump in his throat that never left, even once he landed in Iraq.

## 11

A STRING OF DROOL CONNECTS J.D. TO THE SIDE window of a truck as he opens his eyes. The sun is high in the sky, the snowy weather left behind. For a second he has no idea where he is, still dreaming of the motel room where he last saw Annie. Her long blond hair slipping out the door, her face becoming fuzzier and fuzzier as the years passed, those sweat-soaked sheets of theirs lost forever after the chaos that occurred in Siniyah.

Someone is shaking his shoulder now. He takes in the man's Carolina Panthers cap, the bear cub face, the gap tooth. He realizes that he's far, far away from his past with Annie, the present nothing more than a never-ending trial.

"Time to get in the back, son," Bud says. "Told you come morning I couldn't have anyone seeing you up front."

J.D. slings his backpack over his shoulder. Sleep is calling him to reconvene: menacingly, unrelenting. He's exhausted from the last forty-eight hours, ever since he let the mark go and brought a world of shit to his feet.

Unfortunately, a good night's sleep might be a luxury he'll never have again.

He follows Bud outside, reading the lettering on the guy's truck. *Kamikaze Knives.* A twinge of fear tackles his insides, bats around an organ or two.

"Knives, huh?" he says to Bud, who eyes him carefully.

"Don't get any ideas, grunt."

Bud looks serious, making J.D. wonder if he'd accidently mumbled something defaming in his sleep, an inkling of who he was and the people he's running from. But then Bud lets out a laugh, his bear cub face all smiles again. So J.D. does the same.

"I'll getcha again come sunset," Bud says, opening up the back of the truck. Boxes and boxes of knives. Enough for J.D. to feel their presence, their power.

He steps into the darkness.

"Sweet dreams, son."

Bud shuts the door. There isn't a crack of light to be found.

He'd be completely at the mercy of the Desire Card should its operatives find him and decide to fire a round of bullets into the truck. He contemplates sneaking away; taking his chances with whatever town they just passed through. A night's worth of driving should've brought them somewhere around the edge of the Midwest. A good distance from Gable, but probably not far enough, if anywhere was really far enough.

But even if he wants to run now, his legs don't have it in them. So he fumbles his way over to the stacked crates, positioning himself so he could fall back asleep.

The truck starts up again, the sound of all the knives rattling around. This is a sound he's heard before, oftentimes in the darkness, when sound was all there was to distract him.

In an instant, he nods off again. Although, this time it's to a place he never wants to return.

A Hell he replays in an endless loop.

# 12

THREE WEEKS ON ROTATION IN SINIYAH HAD FELT
like a year. J.D. got used to the bullets whistling through
the sky. Trash was piled up and scattered everywhere,
the stench of a dumpster forever in his nostrils. Crumbling building after crumbling building, each one
littered with bullet holes. Hunting for IEDs, every step
possibly his last, the distance a landscape of mushroom
clouds. His stomach gnawing with hunger, his throat
continually dry, lips chapped and blistered from the
endless sun.

The attacks on coalition forces had gotten worse
since he arrived. A bomb exploded in an umbrella
pattern the other day, wiped out a dozen men. The air
was haunted by the smell of burnt plastic with an
undertone of gunpowder and charred flesh. A skinny
eighteen-year-old in his regiment nicknamed Bean-
pole had survived the blast but the kid's face had
melted, the skin with a gluey consistency that fell off
in clumps. But despite all the horrors J.D. had
witnessed, this was where he was meant to be. He'd

injected Iraq into his veins and war had become some nonstop porn. He'd use his gift to take out every insurgent he could. He'd keep souvenirs of his kills, mementos of his hero status to show his grandkids one day.

Little did he know that his first kill would be his last.

———

The sun had broken along the horizon, the insurgent camp a blurred patchwork of deformed shapes. Perched on a gravel hill, J.D. had just fired a round into a car creeping toward the hideout. His spotter Clinton gave the order and without hesitation J.D. pulled the trigger. The driver collapsed against the car horn, the sound bleating through the dawn like some warped devotional prayer.

He kept his M24 S2S sniper rifle trained on the hideout, waiting for a bad guy to emerge. Out of the corner of his eye, he saw Clinton heading toward the car. A swirl of blood had painted the windshield. Clinton ordered the driver to step outside, his gun peeking through the sheet covering the window.

J.D. turned his attention back to the hideout when a clump of dust spun into his eye, worked its way in good. He took a moment to blink the dirt away, a moment too long.

Gramps had warned him that 'evil won't announce it's coming'.

From behind came the sound of footsteps. He swiveled around as a fist clocked him in the face.

The insurgent had Haji gear wrapped around his

head, just a pair of eyes yelling in a stream of angry Arabic.

J.D. caught bits and pieces of what he was saying: *"May God destroy you. My wife! My son!"*

By the car, he could see Clinton slumped to the ground, his throat slashed, the gash like a mouth spitting up blood.

The insurgent whipped out a gleaming knife with a serrated blade, and J.D. lost his grip on the M24 S2S. The Iraqi pressed the knife close to his face, yelling loud enough to dwarf the pulse of the car horn.

J.D. fought as much as he could, but the sun was starting to cook him, all of his energy nearly zapped. The insurgent danced the edge of the blade over J.D.'s right eye, close enough to swipe an eyelash. J.D. tried to hold the guy back with everything he had in him, but it was no use. The knife slashed across his right eye and he felt liquid pooling from his socket, a parade of never-ending tears.

The insurgent became a blur hovering above him, slowly becoming more and more out of focus.

With his left eye, J.D. spied the M24 S2S. Some deep instinct of survival tore through his belly and gave him the power needed to grab the rifle. He fired one deafening shot. The bullet sailed right through the insurgent's head and became lost in the red sky. The guy's flesh started to singe as he collapsed to the ground with a hole in his head the size of a nickel.

J.D. staggered to his feet, his mouth wide open in shock. He stumbled over to Clinton, whose helmet was rolling by his boot. The pictures of Clinton's wife and kids in Delaware had scattered across the gravel before being picked up by a lone breeze and carried away.

J.D. held up his rifle as he proceeded to the car, the horn still a menace.

He thrust open the driver's side door. A woman fell out like a broken doll. She wore a long *abaya* and *niqaab* over her head, which only allowed her eyes to show. Locked in her arms, she was holding something. He stiffened at the thought that it could be a bomb.

He crouched down and pried her arms open to reveal a dead infant, the head crushed from falling against the steering wheel.

J.D. lost his footing, toppling over and letting out an inhuman scream. The image of the infant seared in his mind, a rotten part of him now.

The world became blurry again. He touched his right eye, slick and syrupy. He realized he wasn't crying tears, but blood, a dark red that almost looked black.

His right eye was hanging out of its socket, swinging like a pendulum.

# 13

In a flea-ridden infirmary, J.D. tapped on his new glass eye. Soldiers in worse shape surrounded him: missing limbs, excessive brain damage, victims of mortar attacks. A tired doctor shuffled over with a slew of documents in his hands. He had the biggest head J.D. had ever seen, as large as a honeydew, or maybe the morphine just hadn't worn off yet.

"You were given an ocular prosthesis," the doctor said. "The prosthesis has been fitted over an orbital implant under the eyelid and is made with cryolite glass. You will not be able to see out of this eye and there is no chance for a visual prosthesis since the nerves were severely damaged."

J.D. just kept tapping.

*Ping. Ping. Ping!*

The doctor handed him the picture of Clinton's wife and kid, thinking it was J.D.'s family. J.D. took it without correcting the doc.

"I also need to tell you, Storm, that you've been recommended for honorable discharge."

J.D. looked up with his good eye, not pleased in the least.

"As a sniper, you had to know this was coming. Your depth perception will be off. There is a support group in your area that I'm going to recommend...."

The doctor continued speaking, but J.D. tuned him out. The one goddamn thing he excelled at, his gift bestowed by the gods had been gouged out. He saw himself becoming one of those vets who couldn't get over their affliction, who were unable to adjust to the real world. Becoming a transient like he did at sixteen when Gramps died, quitting school, ingesting anything he could, hanging out with the worst Newburgh had to offer.

"Consider yourself one of the lucky ones," the doctor said, cracking his knuckles, ready to move onto the next casualty.

"Give me another shot of morphine," J.D. said, grabbing the doctor's arm.

His good eye only showed signs of life once the needle plunged in.

———

All the terrible premonitions J.D. had about his immediate future came true. That first shot of morphine from the doc led to an endless drip. He became a walking IV when he returned home, until the morphine prescriptions ran out and he needed a harder hit to stay numb. Tell yourself not to think about a dead baby with a smashed head, and a tiny cracked skull is all you'll see. At least on heroin the dead baby might give him a break and morph into a rose.

He skipped the support groups. Fuck the support groups. Windows shut, shades taped down, a lighter and corroded spoon in hand while he'd stare at the picture of Clinton's wife and kid. He'd dream of crawling into bed with them, letting this new family soothe his wounds. And then one day or night (he couldn't tell the difference), the picture went up in flames, and the slick spoon clanged to the floor mimicking the sound of a gun's rat-a-tat-tat, and he almost ended himself for good by tossing a bed sheet over the exposed piping in his basement, desperately looking forward to swinging.

A vision of Gramps emerged when J.D. climbed up on a chair and got ready to kick it away. It was the Gramps of his youth, the drill sergeant. The one who'd PT J.D. to death from an early age. Who once strapped a gas mask on J.D. and sent him into a shack filled with CS. The gas mask felt like a plunger, every breath making him winded until Gramps tore it off. Snot poured from J.D.'s nose, his lungs constricted, his eyes licked by flames.

"And what is the soldier's creed?" Gramps yelled.

J.D. managed to spit out: "I am an American soldier...I am disciplined, physically and mentally tough...."

And then Gramps pulled J.D. out of the shack, let him puke up everything inside of him on the lawn, lit up a cigarette and told J.D. he just inhaled modified pepper spray in gaseous form. That he was never in any danger.

"You held onto your mask. You didn't drop it. You did as you should," Gramps said. He wiped the tears pooling from J.D.'s eyes, his fingers rough, but J.D. was glad to be tucked under his arm.

"Let's go hunt us a muley and have a feast."

That day, Gramps gave J.D. his first gun, a sweet rifle handed down by his Pappy. J.D.'s fingers shook as the muley came up in his sights.

"That's it," Gramps cooed. "Track her slow. She's looking left so nudge the rifle a little to the left, then fire."

J.D.'s first shot caught that muley right between her eyes.

After skinning the muley and cooking her over a fire in the backyard, Gramps brought out two mason jars of skim milk with ice. He tapped in some bourbon too. He smiled his yellow smile, teeth gone awry, the bottom row twisted and jagged, as he gnawed at a piece of the muley's rump.

"You'll make a good soldier one day," Gramps sniffed, and chucked a piece of bone in the fire.

Back in the basement, J.D. remembered this as he kicked the chair away and let his feet dangle. The sheet was tight against his neck, digging in and cutting off all circulation. The vision of Gramps disappeared, too ashamed to watch. But then water began spewing from the piping until it loosened from the wall and sent J.D. tumbling down to the floor. He ripped the sheeting from his neck and coughed and coughed, blood vessels popping around his eye sockets. The cold floor soothed his left cheek; rough fingers caressed his other side. Gramps stood before him, drenched.

"You never were no solider if this is how you choose to end."

Gramps balled his hand in a fist and pounded J.D.

in the skull. J.D. took the beating, relished in the pain, licked it up. Finally, Gramps relented and rose on shaking knees.

"Get the help you need," Gramps said. "'Cause I ain't comin' back again."

He punched J.D. one last time and then floated up through the ceiling.

# 14

So J.D. GAVE THE RIDICULOUS SUPPORT GROUP THAT the military recommended a try. Heroin soon started to bore him anyway, and he found himself listening to gruesome tales in the hopes that someone else's pain might supersede his own. They all sat in a circle with a different deformity that made them special. He'd given them nicknames just like he would if he were still in the Army, except these weren't terms of endearment. Giant Goiter. Alopecia. Cleft Palate. No Ears. Woman with a Burned Face. Each one more mopey than the last. Every week a new story of woe.

The only sunny one in the bunch was a Frizzy Haired Lady running the show. She was the worst offender of them all.

Frizzy Hair cleared her throat to begin her spiel.

"As much as someone likes to define you by your deformity, YOUR DEFORMITY IS NOT WHO YOU ARE."

She always liked to punctuate this revelation with a wagging finger.

"OUR DEFORMITIES ARE NOT WHO WE ARE," the group chanted.

J.D. and the Woman with a Burned Face were the only two not chanting the slogan. Burned Face was relatively new to the group, hadn't given her woe saga yet, hadn't broken down in tears. Besides looking like she'd been dipped in scalding oil, she had full lips and silky red hair, the only parts of her face that hadn't been marked.

Frizzy Hair cocked her head at the two of them.

"The healing will only work if you allow yourself to believe in what we're saying."

J.D. and Burned Face eyed each other, both over this group and their preachy bullshit.

"We are not limited by our fears, we are limited by our choices. You are choosing to be afraid," Frizzy Hair added.

"Fuck your slogans," said Burned Face.

"Rita, there's no need to be angry with me–"

"And fuck you. You had tit cancer and they chopped them off. Big deal. No one stares at you on the street like you're a mutant."

"We're not here to compare tragedies."

"Then what the fuck is the point?"

Rita stood up in a huff, knocking her folding chair to the floor. She gave it a look like it deserved its fate and marched out of the room, her high heels firing into the floor.

Alopecia covered her mouth in shock.

Cleft Palate whispered to Giant Goiter.

No Ears glanced around the room, confused as always.

J.D. watched the swish of her nude stockings as she

left. The tiniest smile emerged on his face. The first in a long time.

Impulsively, he got up to chase her down.

The neighborhood outside was a dumping ground for derelicts and bag ladies. The smell of meth in the air, ripe and rancid. He sucked the foulness into his lungs. He found Rita ripping into a cigarette with her back to the building.

"Hey," he said, but she didn't acknowledge him. "Hey! Rita..."

She whipped around, the cigarette pointed at him.

"What the fuck do you want?"

He held up his hands. "A drink. Can I buy you a drink? That's all."

She spat a piece of tobacco at the wind, crossed her arms, and took off down the street.

He followed, unsure if that was her way of saying yes.

———

J.D. and Rita sat across from each other at the saddest diner in existence. Bad lighting, scraps of food congealed on the walls, the seats with gashes like there had been a knife fight, the coffee weak as water.

Rita knocked back the whiskey shot in front of her. She flagged down a waitress in a stained uniform for another.

"So how'd you wind up in that loser support group?" she asked. "Bunch of whiners if you ask me."

She lit a cigarette, her third since they arrived. She liked to smoke only a few puffs worth and then put it out.

"I lost my eye in Iraq."

She offered no condolence, made no attempt to ask how. He continued anyway.

"I dreamed of becoming a soldier when I was a kid. I may have gone astray for a while in my teens, but it's in my blood. I signed up to make a difference. But you can't be a sniper with just one eye."

He tapped on it to show proof. *Ping!*

"Finest glass out there. They call it cryolite. Great for parlor tricks. About all I'm good for now."

She shrugged, unimpressed with his tale.

"My mother was a boozer," she said, crashing the cigarette she just lit into the ashtray. "Bottle of gin every night. Whatever was cheapest. Fell asleep with a cigarette in her bed. Our house went up in flames. She died, the lucky bitch. I'm left to wade in shit."

"How old were you?"

"Old enough to remember what it was like to have a face. I was a cheerleader, took home all the popular boys. After the torching, none of them would even look at me. Mean girls in the halls called me names behind my back. Melty, that was the worst. I quit school, never wound up finishing, sob, sob, sob."

"What about skin grafts?"

"You mean you don't think I got a beautiful face?"

"I–"

"I'm in debt out of my ass."

She lit a new cigarette, took one puff, and then changed her mind.

"Cigarettes aren't cheap, Rita. You might want to finish one."

She sucked at her teeth with a snake-like hiss.

"If I take a puff or two and put it out, I know I won't

fall asleep with it still burning. Force of habit, I guess. And narcolepsy runs in the family."

"I'm in debt, too," J.D. said, spinning an empty coffee mug in his hands and ignoring her sob story. "The bank is about to foreclose on my Gramps' house."

"You mean our wonderful government hasn't compensated you for your eye?"

"Apparently the Armed Forces Compensation Scheme only applies to those injured after April 2005. I missed it by a few weeks."

"Looks like we both got no luck. Besides being a boozer, my sweet mother owed a lot of money to some very bad people. Been paying up ever since. So skin grafts are out of the question. Best I can do for myself is to buy a veil."

A bubble of saliva lingered on the corner of her lip as she glanced at her empty shot of whiskey.

The waitress came by and poured another shot. She went to leave, but Rita held her arm.

"Leave the bottle, honey."

The waitress stared at Rita's face for a second too long, like everyone probably did. She gave a sympathetic nod, as if she understood Rita's need for the entire bottle.

Rita sucked at her teeth again and hissed until the creeped-out waitress sauntered away.

"See how she looks at me? I don't want to be pitied."

"I don't pity you."

She took a shot that looked like it burned as it went down.

"No, I don't think you do."

She traced the rim of the shot glass with a dark fingernail, poured another, and gulped.

"Wanna put a mask over my face and fuck me till I cry?" she asked, taking out one of the last cigarettes in her pack and lighting up. She said it as if she was reading a grocery list.

"I wouldn't want to put a mask over your face," he said, swallowing hard, but he couldn't deny that he was getting aroused.

"It's not about what you want, soldier."

She crashed the cigarette into the ashtray and left the booth in a blink.

He threw some bills on the counter and followed her into the night, a fresh cloud of smoke floating in the air to guide him.

# 15

R ITA LIVED IN A SHIT BOX STUDIO APARTMENT NOT
far from the diner. A bus stop outside her lone window
housed a bag lady curled up with a bottle of cheap
vodka like it was her teddy bear. The walls were thin
enough to hear the neighbors fighting in Spanish. The
kitchen sink overflowed with crusted dishes and wet
cigarette butts. In the corner, a halogen lamp cast an
orange sheen over her bed, the sheets unmade. In
another life, J.D. would've had the urge to clean the
place obsessively, tuck those sheets in military style; but
now he felt at home in all that filth.

"Sorry I didn't have time to tidy up," she said, sitting
on the bed and sliding off her nude stockings.

"It's a...nice place you got."

She laughed but it sounded more like a cough.

"Open the bottom shelf of that drawer for me."

She pointed to a bureau. He crouched down and
did as he was told. The drawer had been filled with
masks, most of them cheap plastic knockoffs like the
ones little kids wore on Halloween.

"Any preference?" he asked, picking up a Minnie Mouse mask.

"Should be a Rita Hayworth in there," she said. "You know who that is?"

"Of course I do. I was raised on old movies like *Gilda*."

He pulled out a mask that sort of resembled Rita Hayworth. Plastic red hair, killer smile, except the eyes were hollow. He held it up to make sure it was the one she wanted.

"Let's go, soldier," she said, patting the messy sheets. "I'm ready to start crying."

He walked over to the bed and she yanked the mask from his hands. She put it on and immediately began to take off her clothes, her body quite lovely. Pale skin, but not translucent or veiny, cream-colored and smooth. The fire had only destroyed her face.

"Call me Rita Hayworth when you fuck me. Not just Rita. I don't want to be her right now."

He unbuckled his pants and whipped off his shirt. Her tongue slithered through the mask's mouthpiece and licked his nipple, then bit down. She slid off his boxers and shoved him inside of her as they flopped onto the bed.

"Say my name," she cried.

"Rita...oh yeah.... Yeah, Rita..."

"My whole name, motherfucker! You say my whole name!"

She wrapped her hands around his neck and began to choke him.

"Rita...Hayworth," he gasped.

"That's right," she hissed, a tear dripping down the mask's cheek. "That's motherfucking right."

———

Ten minutes later he had finished and was cleaning himself up in the bathroom. Through the medicine cabinet he could see her lounging in bed, naked with the mask still on. She had an ashtray on her belly with two cigarettes already put out. She puffed at her third and then crashed it amongst the rest.

The last girl he'd been with was Annie. When he first got to Iraq, some guys had found a whorehouse in a nearby village but he didn't participate. He could still feel Annie then: the tangy taste of her skin, her lemony smell. He didn't want that muddled by some other random girl. Now she was gone for good.

After he was discharged, he thought about contacting her. He didn't have a number or an exact address, but he could've found her if he really wanted. Was he too embarrassed for losing his eye and being shipped home like a lame dog? He didn't know. He just knew he wasn't ready to be happy yet. He wanted to abuse himself a little longer. Rita seemed like the type that could help him out with that. They could abuse one another.

He left the bathroom and joined her on the bed, caressing the mask.

"I'm gonna get a real one soon," she said.

He propped himself up on his elbow. "What do you mean?"

"A real mask. Human hair and everything. Contours to your face perfectly. Looks exactly like Rita Hayworth."

"What for?"

"Because I'll hopefully be an operative soon, no

longer a trainee," she said, as if he had any clue what she was talking about.

"This is for your job? What do you do?"

She breathed heavy through her nostrils.

"What don't I do is a better question."

She lit another cigarette and blew an O at her cottage cheese ceiling.

"So what do you do now that you're not a soldier anymore?"

"Perfecting the art of suicide."

"What if I said I might have a job for you? The organization I work for is looking for the emotionless type."

"How can you be sure that's me?"

"I can see it in your eye. Hard to tell which is your good one. Both got a gaze like ice."

"I've seen a lot of terrible things."

"So have all the trainees. That's how the Boss likes them."

"He rehabilitates people?"

She didn't answer that. She put out her cigarette, leaned in close, and planted a kiss on his lips.

"What's this organization all about?"

"Why don't I let my Boss tell you more? I can introduce you. I think it'll be worth your while."

She lay back, spread her legs, and called him over with a curl of her index finger.

"But I need you to fuck me again first. I'm not done crying yet."

# 16

RITA'S BOSS HAD AN OFFICE BUILT FOR A GOD seventy stories high in New York City. A skyline panorama on par with the top of the Empire State Building, the people below nothing more than tiny bugs. Paintings of swirls on the walls that probably cost millions. A giant wet bar with bottles of top shelf liquor. The head of a steer mounted over the guy's desk along with an old timey rifle that likely caused the animal's demise.

The Boss stood with his back to them, gazing at his spectacular view.

"Knock," said Rita.

The Boss swiveled around wearing a Clark Gable mask. This wasn't a cheap Halloween knockoff like Rita had, the mask looked real enough to believe that Clark Gable had risen from the dead to greet them. Just like she described, it contoured his face perfectly, the material like actual skin, the hair definitely human. The only thing that made it seem otherworldly was a speaker box inconspicuously implanted in the mouthpiece.

Clark Gable looked physically fit, but J.D. guessed him to be an older man, mid to late sixties. He wore a tailored suit and had a smoking Cuban in his hand. He oozed persona and confidence, owning every room he entered. J.D. pictured the guy surrounded by employees who hung on his every word, who quaked from his presence, this Boss with a capital B.

"Welcome," Gable said, taking a drag of the cigar through the mask. The speaker in the mouthpiece altered his voice so it sounded robotic.

"J.D. Storm, sir."

Gable shook his hand and gave a tight squeeze to show who the alpha was.

"Rita said she'd be bringing someone in," he replied, finally ending the handshake that had crushed a few of J.D.'s digits.

"Yeah, she mentioned that you might be looking to hire someone. I could use the work."

Gable didn't reply right away, as if he was considering the question worthy.

"I run a very elite organization," he finally said. "We don't hire just anyone. But if one of our own gives a recommendation, I make sure to listen."

"Why the masks?" J.D. asked, wanting to touch Gable's face and see how real it felt.

"This organization isn't my only business so I like to keep my identity a mystery. I prefer that all of my operatives do the same."

J.D. could hear Rita sucking at her teeth. He didn't know if this was just a habit of hers, or if she wanted to show her displeasure for having not risen in the ranks yet.

"Might J.D. and I talk in private?" Gable asked her,

his robotic voice with more of a menacing tone than before.

"Certainly," Rita said, lowering her head. This was a different woman than J.D. had just been with. Subservient. Even fearful. A tremble in her bottom lip as she sauntered away.

"Lovely girl," Gable said, once she had left. "Terrible shame. But once I make her an operative, she'll never have to show her burned face again. She can feel complete."

"You'll give her a Rita Hayworth mask?"

Gable touched his nose.

"Smart fellow here. I'm surprised you know of the screen legend. We live in an unfortunate time right now, not like when I was a child. Our celebrities, our idols, are not what they used to be. We are celebrated for being public nuisances or sex tape provocateurs. But few have ever been more stunning than Rita Hayworth. Sad to say but the majority of men your age probably couldn't pick her out of a lineup."

"I was raised on old movies by my Gramps."

"And your parents?"

J.D. took a second before responding, the words phlegmy in his throat.

"Their car...hit a bad patch of black ice when I was a toddler. Don't remember them much. Bits and pieces maybe, but that's probably just from old photographs. By the time I was sixteen, Gramps had died and I was on my own."

"I think I have the perfect mask for you," Gable said. He went over to a closet and searched through a row of masks set upon the top shelf. Jimmy Stewart. Cary Grant. Marlon Brando. James Cagney. Rita

Hayworth at the end looked the realest of them all, as if her head had been cut off and preserved. Finally, Gable found a James Dean mask tucked in the back. He handed it to J.D.

"James Dean?"

"You have the hint of a rebel in you," Gable said. "I can tell."

J.D. eyed the mask suspiciously, but he couldn't deny that he was intrigued. He hadn't felt intrigued about anything since he returned from Iraq. Anything beyond a bottle to crawl into, or a hit of something foul to knock him into oblivion.

"So what does your organization do?"

Gable handed over a crisp white business card from his inside jacket pocket.

### THE DESIRE CARD
*Any wish fulfilled for the right price*
PRESS below to inquire

"The Desire Card?" J.D. said, scrunching up his face.

"We are that magical genie in a lamp. Whatever you desire, we can grant. We never judge and nothing is outside our ethical boundaries."

"And what do your masked men do?"

"They facilitate these wishes. Sometimes they must be willing to toe the line as well."

"What does that mean?"

J.D. could see a trace of a smile through Gable's mouthpiece.

"A client's wish is paramount, all else is superfluous."

"And what do you do?"

"I make sure everything runs smoothly."

J.D. tapped his index finger against the card, considering the pitch.

"What's the pay?"

Gable touched his nose again. "I like the way you think. Money is really all that matters in the end."

"How do you even know I'm right for the job?"

"You fit the profile of what we're looking for. I like former soldiers since they know how to follow orders."

"How'd you know I was in the Army?"

"Support groups like yours are usually full of ex-grunts, the newly deformed."

"You mean you recruited me? I only served a few weeks in Iraq. Why would you want a useless soldier like me?"

Gable nodded at J.D.'s index finger that was twitching like crazy.

"You never got to see your marksmen talents put to good use. This can allow you to be a part of something again."

J.D. grabbed hold of his twitching trigger finger, trying to keep it steady.

"What would you need a marksman for?"

"Often times people's wishes are in the vein of the extraordinary. The finest cigars in existence for example, Gurkha Black Dragons. The Desire Card can make that happen within the hour. But once in a while people wish for things a little more...suspect. And like I said, we make no judgments and promise *any* wish fulfilled. Our clients rely on that mantra."

"You mean you hire hit men–"

Gable held up his palm, expecting silence.

"I began this organization to make my clients' lives a little more special, Mr. Storm. These are CEOs, world-class athletes, powerful politicians. You have to reach a certain level to even be shown this card. These are men and women who usually get whatever they desire, but there is always that elusive wish out there, the one we keep secret, the one we don't believe is possible. Throughout my years, there has never been a desire I haven't fulfilled."

"You still haven't told me the pay."

"A straight shooter," Gable laughed, the sound like a machine gun. "I like that. In terms of pay, I have a cottage that's become available in Vermont. And you tell me what your price is. I'm known to give my employees whatever it is they deserve. Of course, if you excel with us and make it to operative status, you'll receive even more. Plus some perks."

"You know my depth perception is off because of my missing eye?"

"I know all about you. And I don't care. I believe you still got it."

"And what if I don't?"

"We'll cross that bridge when we reach it. You'll start out as a trainee like everyone else, but I have a feeling you're going to stick around a while."

"The Desire Card, huh?"

J.D. glanced at the card again. Clean and crisp: sharp lettering, blinding white stock, metallic feel.

"What the fuck do I have to lose, I guess?" he said, half to Gable and half to himself.

"Good to hear."

They shook hands again, although this time J.D. wasn't about to let his be crushed. He squeezed as hard as he could until the handshake became a test of wills that neither man would back down from. Finally, they each let go at the same moment, both clearly in pain but neither allowing the other to see any weakness.

"Welcome to your future, soldier," Gable said, turning towards his panoramic view. "Be sure to have one of my assistants outside set everything up."

J.D. rubbed his throbbing hand, backing up towards the door. He could've sworn he saw Gable clench his fist, as if the Boss was trying to crush all of the tiny bugs seventy stories below.

## 17

J.D. WAKES UP IN THE DARKNESS, SWEAT SOAKING his collar, no idea where he is. The sounds of knives rattling around bring him back to reality. He's still in Bud's truck, no clue if it's night or day, if Killenroy is in reach or if they're a long way off. Bud might've been eliminated and an operative could be manning the wheel. They could even be driving back to one of the Desire Card's headquarters in far-out New Jersey to properly torture him for his disobedience.

The truck comes to a stop as the knives quiet down.

He hears the front door slam. One of the crates he's sitting on is slightly ajar so he pries it open and pulls out a knife. He stuffs it in the inside pocket of his coat.

The back door opens with a bang, letting in a flood of light. Bud stands there in the morning sun.

J.D. runs his fingers over the knife's handle.

"Christ, son, you've been out like a light for more than a day. Tried to wake you come dark last night to give ya a sandwich, but you weren't having it." He eyes

J.D. closely. "You were sure talkin' up a storm in your sleep."

"What was I saying?"

"Lots of things. First about some girl...Rita, I think. That ain't the one you're sweet on, is it? Then I heard ya saying that—"

"Why did you stop the truck now?" J.D. asks, still fingering the knife's handle.

"Can't you see, son?" Bud gestures towards the wilderness. "You in Killenroy. I can almost see Canada past them forests."

Hesitantly, J.D. steps out of the truck with his backpack slung over his shoulder. The area is a nature lover's wet dream, an endless view of green trees and mountains.

"I told ya I'd take ya all the way," Bud says. He slaps J.D. on the back, which causes the knife to slip out of the coat pocket and fall to the ground.

J.D. stares at the spinning knife, a million possible outcomes flashing through his skull: grabbing the knife and plunging it into Bud's neck, holing out in the woods in the back of the guy's truck long enough for Gable to forget about him.

Finally, Bud lets out a hoarse laugh.

"I'm goin' let you have it, son. That wound on your ear wasn't from rollin' down no hill. Someone did that to you."

J.D. bends down and picks up the knife.

"Thanks for driving me all this way," he says, unzipping the backpack to toss in the knife. Immediately he notices that his 9mm gun is missing and his limbs go cold. He longs for the feel of it in his hands: the heaviness, the warmth.

"Lookin' for this?" Bud asks, removing the gun from his flannel.

J.D. still has his hand in the backpack, the knife within reach.

Bud gestures with the gun.

"Lemme see some hands, come on there."

J.D. removes his hand from the backpack and reaches for the sky.

"There's not much I have for you to take–"

"I looked through your pack already. Saw some bills, but I left them."

"I need that gun, Bud."

"Son, we can't run from our problems for too long. They gonna catch up soon enough."

"Which is why I can't let you take my gun."

"I'm aware you've done some things in your days," Bud says. "Things you're ashamed of, things that can be considered evil. You've killed people, I heard ya in your sleep. And not just in war, you killed for a living after you returned home. Can't have you out there with no gun. Wouldn't be right."

"But you let me keep the knife?"

"Knives ain't the same. Knives don't take innocent lives as much. My baby girl Lacey was shot on the playground in '79 by a stray bullet. No more than six-years-old. They never found the killer or why someone was firing around a kid's school. Turned my wife into a crazy woman, God bless her. She's finally at peace now. Been at an institution in Raleigh for twenty some years. Guns ain't the answer, son."

"But I'm being hunted."

"Just got a find another way to outsmart them then.

I ain't letting you go with this gun. My baby girl don't deserve that."

"You'll be sealing my fate."

"Your fate will eventually be sealed anyway for what you've done. God don't let sinners slip through the cracks. He's already decided when your time is coming, gun or not."

"I'm not the man that killed your daughter."

"No, but you're all the same. And someone innocent is bound to be caught in the crosshairs."

Bud spits a wad of chew to the pavement and backs up toward his truck, the gun still pointed.

J.D. runs a few scenarios in his head. He could lunge at Bud and hope the bullet doesn't connect. He could whip out the knife and fling it between the old man's eyes.

Bud is crying, quiet manly tears. This guy has already been utterly destroyed, but J.D. finds himself unable to attack him for a different reason. So he lets Bud hop back in the truck and drive off down the road.

The moment the truck vanishes in the distance, J.D. curses under his breath for having a heart, for not thinking about himself first. As he walks past a sign that says Welcome to Killenroy, Pop. 5,120, he promises only to be selfish when he arrives in town, for Killenroy needs to be his home for a while until he can scrape up enough cash to truly disappear. He knows he won't stand a chance unless he removes anyone primed to take him down, or even someone standing in his way, regardless of whether they resemble Gramps a little like Bud did.

He should've gotten his gun back no matter what.

From now on, he'll make sure not to listen to his pestering conscience anymore, at least until he's far enough away to stay hidden for his remaining days.

Then he can work on becoming human once again.

# PART TWO
## GUN. CASH. ADIOS.

# 18

KILLENROY HAS THE VIBE OF A RUN-DOWN TOWN, different than J.D. remembers from years ago. Since he's traveled the world now, he wonders if that's the reason it seems so abandoned, or if it's inevitably become like his hometown Newburgh and any other blip across the country—fucked by the spiraling economy and full of jobless addicts.

As he walks through, Killenroy's few people seemed removed from time, stuck in the past. Their clothes steeped in the 1980s but not with a retro look, hand-me-downs that have withered over generations. Mullets galore, both on the men and the women. Tough blue-collar types with chaw in their cheeks, already plastered at this hour of the morning. Tweakers and meth-heads oozing from the street cracks, gummy eyes unpleased with a new arrival on their turf. And off in the distance, the greenest trees he's ever seen, a forest hugging the area and keeping it isolated in its own bubble.

At the end of Main Street sits the Border Diner, the "B" barely hanging onto the signpost.

———

The time warp continues as J.D. enters the Border Diner. Waitresses with tall hair and heavy make-up in baby blue uniforms. Tubular neon lights in diamond patterns buzzing from the ceiling. A red and white-checkered floor with a ring of stools around the counter. Hardly any customers keeping the place afloat except for a fat man dripping off one of the stools and tearing into a generous piece of lemon pie.

A country crooner warbles from the jukebox.

> *"Yesterday is dead and gone,*
> *and tomorrow's out of sight.*
> *And it's sad to be alone.*
> *Help me make it through the night."*

J.D. takes the stool next to the fat man who is unconcerned with anything but his pie.

An older waitress shuffles by: gray hair in a bun, horse teeth, even her wrinkles have wrinkles. She eyes J.D. up and down, doesn't seem to like what she sees.

"What can I get ya?"

"Cup of coffee and can I use your bathroom?"

"Don't need my permission."

She shuffles away.

In the bathroom, J.D. stands in front of a crusty mirror. His ear isn't looking too good, the dried blood turned blackish. He wets a paper towel and cleans it as much as he can.

"Am I crazy to look up Annie like this?" he asks the filthy mirror. "What are the chances she's even still living here? How can she possibly save me? How can anyone save me now?"

He tosses the bloody wad at the garbage, misses.

When he returns to the counter, the older waitress is about to pour his coffee.

"Let me ask you something, miss?"

She barely glances up.

"I'm passing through here. Thought I'd see if an old friend still lives in these parts. Annie Duluth, you know her?"

The waitress licks the lipstick stain off her teeth.

"Yeah, I know her. Hoity-toity skinny little blond thing. Worked here some years back. Didn't last more than a month. Thought she was better than this place. Always had her nose to the sky."

"She still live in town?"

"Yeah, she's still here. See her around from time to time turning up her nose like always. Hope a birdie craps on it one day."

The waitress lets out a deflated laugh.

"You know, I bet that girl's just been waiting for some eye-patch-wearing, bloody ear kind-of-fella to come and sweep her off her feet."

J.D. throws a ten on the counter, no time for sarcasm.

"Just tell me where she lives and keep the change."

The fat man reaches over and grabs the ten between his sticky fingers.

"Girl lives on Old Stanton Drive," the fat man wheezes. "Last house before the dead end."

"Goddamn, Sam, that ten dollars was my ticket out of this piss hole."

The waitress gives J.D. a wink as she finishes pouring his cup, the coffee thick as mud.

# 19

WALKING UP TO ANNIE'S HOUSE, J.D. PASSES A FEW other homes randomly scattered along old Stanton Drive, each of them in varying stages of disrepair. At the front yard of a particularly grotesque one, a mangy mutt runs in circles trying in vain to catch its tail, its teeth snapping at the air. The dog pauses from its pursuit to growl at J.D. One of its eyes has closed over just like his, probably due to a nasty fight. J.D. leans back on his haunches ready for the dog should it attack, but the mutt resumes chasing its tail, spinning around and kicking up a dirt storm like some Tasmanian devil.

Annie's sad shack of a house waits at a dead end, the forest her backyard. The area is devoid of life, eerie and silent, except for the realized image of Ouroboros in the form of a dog, still intent on catching its tail. Finally, the mutt sinks its teeth in and lets out a howl.

He knocks on Annie's door. No answer. Knocks again, this time a little more forceful.

The whimpering dog has curled into a ball, licking its wounds.

"Hold on, I'm comin'," Annie yells from inside.

The sound of her voice hits him instantly, wrangles his heart. That twangy Southern drawl, how she often stressed the first part of each word. Her accent isn't as pronounced as he remembers it to be, but it's still there.

The door flings open. Annie stands behind the screen door, pretty as she ever was. Blonde, tawny hair, styled a little messy and tucked back behind her ears. A slightly upturned nose just like the old waitress at the Border Diner had described, something he hadn't noticed before. Just a trace of lipstick, since a girl like her doesn't need to paint on too much make-up. She could still pass for ten years younger, but her face has hardened some: frown lines more apparent, eyes steely and untrusting. *Who's this fucker at my door?* those eyes ask. *And what the hell could he possibly want?*

"Yeah, can I help you?"

"Is the eye-patch throwing you, Annie?"

She looks him up and down.

"Holy shit...J.D.? Motherfucking J.D.?"

She stumbles a bit but catches herself on the doorframe.

"What the...what're you...? Well, come in, come in. Don't stand there out in the cold."

She bangs open the screen door.

He gives one last glance at Old Stanton Drive. There's still no sign of anyone following him, just the dog with a bloody tongue from lapping at its tail.

———

Stepping inside, there's a lemony smell in the air. It takes J.D. right back to eight years ago. Annie's place is sparse but homey: an old television with a dial, knick-knacks on the fireplace mantle, a couple of framed pictures along the walls. She gives a shrug as if she's embarrassed by the décor, but he has the overwhelming sensation of never wanting to leave. To spend the rest of his days in its comfort until old age takes them both.

"I wasn't sure you'd remember me," he says, as she disappears into the kitchen.

"Wasn't sure you remembered me either," she shouts back. "I'm just getting us some drinks."

He looks at the pictures on her walls. One shows a tough Annie surrounded by a bunch of bikers with the forest as a backdrop. Another depicts a pigtailed little girl wearing a ladybug costume, her tiny fingers with chipped nail polish, her two front teeth missing.

Annie returns from the kitchen with two glasses and a bottle of bourbon.

"Now I know it's only two in the afternoon, but I think this calls for somethin' stiff."

She pours two finger's worth in each and hands him a glass.

"Cheers," he says, as they both take a few sips and sit down.

"My mind is racing," she says, shaking her head. "In a million years, I never would've thought you'd be in my living room, J.D. What're you doing here?"

He looks to the right, unsure how much to say. Telling her the whole truth is certainly out of the question, but giving her a small grain might be smarter than a bag of lies.

"I was passing through Washington–"

"I didn't mean to give you the third degree or nothin'."

She crosses her legs, causing a bit of bourbon to slosh around the glass and spill on her dress.

"Look at me, I'm nervous as ever."

"No, I get it, Annie. Like, what the fuck am I doing here, right? But I was passing through Washington and... I don't know, I just thought of you."

She eyes him carefully, hard to tell whether she believes him or not.

"You thought of me?"

"I mean...I've thought of you before...from time to time."

She gives a half-smile, genuinely touched. She runs a finger around the edge of her glass, the nail polish chipped just like the little girl's in the ladybug picture.

"It's been what...like...seven years, J.D.?"

"Eight," he says, a little too quickly.

She cocks her head to one side. "Okay, eight years then. A long while at least."

A whistling sound escapes from her nose. She pinches the bridge. She's looking at him like she's imagining what their life would've been like if he never left for the war, or at least that's what he's telling himself.

"You know when I got to Iraq, I sometimes wondered if you ever wrote me a letter." He glances at his glass of bourbon, getting lost in the swill of liquid. "I pictured that letter traveling all the way there and then becoming stuck in some crumbling post office until it got blown to pieces. That sounds weird, huh?"

He laughs but he doesn't have enough in him to make the laugh stick; it dies out before it really starts.

"It's not weird. I actually did write you a letter once. Swear to it. Couldn't sleep one night and put down an opus. Even got out the address you gave me, fixed it with a stamp and all."

"But you never sent it?"

The corner of her mouth settles back into a frown.

"I met someone soon after you left town. Got married with a kid on the way and everythin'."

He wonders if he missed seeing a picture of that hubby and a kid. Maybe the little girl in the ladybug costume was actually her daughter? He debates if maybe he should just go.

"You have a kid," he nods. "Sure...well, I bet you're a great mom."

She knocks back the rest of her bourbon.

"I had a miscarriage."

"I'm sorry to hear that."

"No, I was young and wild and not ready anyway. Would've been a disaster."

"And your husband?"

She reaches for the bottle. "He was pretty cruel. Not abusive or nothin'...well, not physically at least. Just a lot of calling me 'shit for brains, fuck face', stuff like that."

"I'm glad you got out of that relationship then."

"You'd think so. Not much has changed since. Most of the men around here are like that. Loggers and drinkers."

She gnaws at the corner of her lip, the flesh a little raw, a sad habit.

"You seeing someone now?" he asks.

"There's this guy Abram. On and off kind of thing. What day is it today? Wednesday?"

"Couldn't tell you."

"Yeah, middle of the week we're usually off again.

Weekend he comes 'round. He's at a job across the border now. We'll figure it out when he gets back."

"Well, you look great. Seriously. The years have been...really good to you."

"Least they've been good for something."

He doesn't know what to say to that.

"And you, J.D.? You still in the Army? What happened to your eye?" Immediately she covers her mouth. "That's so rude of me. I didn't mean to–"

"No, it's all right. Souvenir from Iraq. Got me discharged."

She pours herself another drink. He tells her to top him off as well.

"I remember how much being a soldier meant to you."

"It did, but that's far in the past."

"It's just crazy you're sitting in front of me, J.D. Storm. I'm honestly blown over."

He stares at the bourbon in his hand again, twitches his nose.

"I haven't been completely honest with you about why I'm here."

"Yeah, I figured so."

"I got into trouble with the wrong kind of people back east."

She doesn't react, just continues sipping her bourbon.

"Anyway, Annie, I'm looking to go really far away, remote island kind of deal. But I need to lay low for a while. Make some quick money for a plane ticket and a fake passport first. Then I'll head to an airport when I feel like the time is right."

She lets out a laugh that's more like a sigh.

"And you thought a girl like me would know a way to make that happen?"

She taps the glass with a fingernail: part of her ashamed, part of her proud.

"Look, there's no way these wrong-kind-of-people know I'm out here in Killenroy. Not for a while at least. But I don't want to bring trouble to your door. If you want me to leave I will."

Annie smiles, the first full one she's given him since he arrived.

"Hell, J.D., trouble's all I know. What's a little more?"

# 20

AFTER A FEW HOURS OF CATCHING UP, DUSK HAS settled in and J.D. and Annie have migrated to the couch. The bourbon she brought out is half-empty. For the first time in a long while, he allows himself to bask in the present, to take pleasure in this girl he once adored, to enjoy his inebriated state without a pressing need to look over his shoulder. The hunt will resume tomorrow, but for tonight, let him pretend he inhabits a different body. A man can only take so much before he destructs.

Annie has loosened up as well. She's taken off her shoes, put her bare feet up on the coffee table, her toenails done in a dark red. She's told him about a litany of exes from her former husband to the current guy, an endless circle of son-of-a-bitches. Along with being unlucky in love, she's had a string of jobs that have led nowhere. Right now, she's got a telemarketing gig she can do from home.

"I'm that person who calls and talks to you about

switching your insurance. You know, the one you hang up on?"

The bourbon makes him realize how much he's missed alcohol over these last few days of flight, the wonder of its sting on his lips. He had gotten used to demolishing a bottle of Scotch after every finished job, unsatisfied until his head was in the toilet puking up every last organ. Until he could feel nothing.

"Sometimes if it's a man on the other line, they won't hang up," Annie continues. "They like the sound of my voice, want me to talk about anythin'. I've had requests for phone sex before, but since the calls are monitored, I have to remain polite and stick to the script. Those men don't make me angry though. They just get me thinkin' that maybe I should put my voice to better use."

She crosses her legs and he can't help but stare. He blinks and he finds himself running his palm up that smooth leg, peeling back her dress, falling into her arms. He blinks again and sadly realizes that it was just a fantasy.

"What would your boyfriend think about you going into the sex operator biz?"

"Oh Abram? He's the kind of guy to get turned on. Talkin' dirty is what he does. But he's the jealous type, too."

"What would he think about me being here right now?"

She bites her lip. "Oh, I dunno, maybe rough you up a bit. Bruise that good-looking face of yours."

"So, you think I'm good looking?"

"You know you are, J.D. It's them silent types that

gets us girls crazy. We're all dying to know what's going on in that head of yours. For example, you haven't told me nothin' of what you've been doing since the Army. You've just let me run my mouth the whole afternoon."

"I've been working for this...organization."

"Are these the people you're running from?"

He touches his nose, a very Gable-like gesture. Immediately after doing so, he hates himself and wants to take it back.

"What did you do for this organization?" she asks, titillated. He can see it in her eyes: the excitement, the dangerous possibilities.

"I facilitated people's darkest wishes," he says, clearing his throat.

"Sounds mysterious."

"If only it was that."

"And now you don't want to do this anymore?"

He goes to touch his nose again and then stops himself. He listens to the wind outside, the only sound besides the two of them. It's too quiet, and he can feel his stomach turning.

"I shouldn't say anything else. If these people ever caught up to me, if they found you...it's best if you don't know anything."

"Oh, J.D.," she laughs. "I'm a big girl and can handle it. How about you tell me just a nugget and I'll make sure to hook you up with Abram. He's got a so-called crew in town. Odd scams here and there. Always in and out of jail but—"

"You can do so much better. I hope you realize that."

"I don't want to be having that conversation now."

He holds up his hands, giving in so she'll continue.

"Anyway, when Abram comes back from Canada he's bound to have some scheme that you could get in on."

"That'd be great. Really, really great."

The two stare at each other, the sexual tension obvious. To avoid it, he offers up a grain of truth for her to nibble on.

"Sometimes our darkest wishes can be beautiful," he says, as a foreign entity lingers at the corner of his good eye—an actual tear. He strains his facial muscles to hold it back. "When I first started at the organization, I was given the case of a wife whose older husband was dying from a fatal disease. He'd been kept as a vegetable at a hospital for years because her stepchildren didn't want to pull the plug, but that was what he wished for. He had told her this before slipping into a coma, however they hadn't gotten a chance to put it in his will. Since his children wouldn't listen to reason, she finally contacted us."

Annie tucks her legs close to her chest as if a chill has entered the house.

"Do you want me to continue?" he asks, afraid to look her in the eye.

She nods, transfixed.

"I broke into the hospital late at night and unplugged the life-support machines, watched as he took his last breath. When I think back to it, the guy always has a smile on his face. I know that's impossible, but that's how I choose to remember it."

"How did it feel?" Annie gulps.

"What do you mean?"

"To take someone's life, to watch it slip away?"

"I had done it before in Iraq."

"Is that why you got that tattoo?"

She nods at the quote on his forearm from *The Call of the Wild* written in a graffiti style:

```
"Kill  or  be  killed,  eat  or  be
eaten,  was  the  law;  and  this
mandate,  out  of  the  depths  of
Time, he obeyed."
```

"No, I got this more recently," he says, tracing the letters. He thinks of the girl in the alleyway in New York City who Bogart knocked out because it was someone's gruesome wish. He wonders if she's still alive. But he can't worry about her for too long, not unless he wants to have a breakdown. He needs to direct his mind to something else.

The wind has stopped beating against the house. He becomes aware of the silence, of the miniscule distance between he and Annie, her foot just millimeters away. She's breathing heavily, a mixture of fear and lust. He doesn't know which way the scale tips between the two, or if it even matters. Finally, she glances out of the window, inches even closer to him to do so.

"Damn, it's dark out already."

"Yeah," he replies, getting his bearings. "Look at that."

"You should stay here. Only motel in town is bound to have bedbugs. I got a guest room."

"What about Abram?"

"What about Abram? He ain't here now."

She grabs the glass of bourbon from him and places it on the coffee table. Then she takes his hand.

"Have you been lonely, J.D.? I have."

She slides up against him, her lips grazing his cheek.

"Annie, I–"

She's delicate at first, a peck on his earlobe, his body buzzing, yearning. A dot of sweat on her upper lip that he kisses, sugary and salty at the same time. She pulls him to his feet as they drunkenly fondle each other, tearing off clothes, sucking at every body part in reach.

"Take me to the bedroom," she says.

He lifts her up. She wraps her legs around him, knocking the bottle of bourbon to the floor. Fumbling into the bedroom, J.D.'s an animal that's been caged. He throws her onto the bed, dives in. She pulls down his pants and slips off her underwear, red like he remembered them being when they first met.

"You don't have to worry, I'm on the pill."

He starts fucking her madly, the past few days having taken its toll. For a moment, she's everything; all else disappears. He cries into her hair, letting his tears mix with sweat. She's got her eyes shut tight, moaning at the moon outside. He fucks her as if his body is filled with poison and she's the only chance for a sweet release.

Once they come, he remains inside of her, not wanting to pull out, to end this break from reality. He tucks his nose into the nape of her neck and takes in a whiff of lemon, locks it in his memory this time for good.

Finally, he rolls off of her and stares at the cracks of the ceiling.

"The last time I was with you was the last time I truly felt like I had my whole life ahead of me."

He turns to her, wanting to be exposed.

"In some bizarro world, I could've just been content with someone like you. Never joined up with the Desire Card, never let Gable's money drive me, never been responsible for ending so many lives. I could've been happy."

"What's that?" she asks, because he hadn't said those words out loud, only imagined them.

"I was just thinking about the last eight years. What could've been?"

"I don't play that game. Regret? That's a box I never need to open."

He kisses her again, softly now. Strokes her hair and stares into her eyes to get lost for one last time.

———

The next morning, J.D. wakes up alone in Annie's bedroom, the sun flitting through the blinds. He hears murmurs from outside the door and realizes he's left his backpack with the knife in the living room. He grabs her alarm clock to use as a weapon instead.

Annie comes in wearing a pink negligee, her hair tousled.

"Lookin' to cause some damage with that alarm clock?"

He puts it down, hesitantly. "My nerves are still a little fried."

She sits on the bed.

"So, Abram just called. You'll like this, he told me

he's planning some new scheme when he's back in Killenroy."

"What is it?"

"He don't ever tell me details. But I'll talk you up. He'll like that you're an ex-Army sniper. I know he's always lookin' for crack shots."

"Thank you, Annie."

"It's nothing."

"You didn't tell him my name yet, did you?"

"No, just mentioned that I knew of someone looking in his line of work."

"Marcus Edmonton, that's my name if he asks."

"Okay...Marcus."

She wrings her hands and shifts uncomfortably in place.

"J.D., I don't know how to say this the right way, but what happened between you and me last night can never happen again. I want to make it work with Abram. I do. You just...you were here...and it was lovely."

"It was."

"But now you got to go to the bedbug motel. We're gonna be at Trigger Happy tonight. Yeah, that place still exists. You can meet Abram and his crew then."

She gets up to leave, but he grabs her arm.

"One more time for the road?" he asks, desperate for another hit of her fantasy.

"Honey, I might not be able to let you go if we do that again."

"So?"

"Tell me about that remote island you wanted to run away to. What was it called?"

"The name doesn't matter," he says. "Just picture paradise."

"Don't really have much to draw from."

She kisses him on the forehead and heads into the bathroom.

"I'm turning on the shower for you," she calls out.

And then in a whisper, he hears her add, "Needs some time to warm up."

# 21

Tucked beneath a patch of pine trees is the Bedbug Motel. Its actual name is the Bed Rest Motel but Bedbug sums it up better since it seems like an insect army calls it home. The lobby is all plywood and plaid couches, steeped in dust and ruin. The curtains covering the windows look chewed up by moths. An area rug squishes when stepped on. Behind the front desk, a squat woman with a midsection like she swallowed a tire hands J.D. a key, no electric cards here.

His room is even worse. Wooden walls thin enough to put your fist through, questionable stains aplenty and an old TV with a tube that only shows snow. He flops down on a mattress that takes its last dying breath, then opens his backpack and removes the Kamikaze Knife.

Running his index finger over the blade, he gets philosophical: what led him to this moment? The choices that one makes. How life can twist and turn without warning. And a memory of Annie writhing above him, his hands on her hips as he thrust until morning came.

But he can't let himself lose focus. Getting a gun should be his primary concern, since it's just a matter of time before the Card finds him. There's even a chance they're already here watching him squirm. Gable enjoys playing games, especially with someone who defied him more than once. The first strike had been with the girl in the alleyway. Since most operatives never stuck around long enough to make a second mistake, Gable might be getting creative with J.D.'s demise.

He could recall an unfortunate Spencer Tracy, a recent trainee who threatened to sell everything he knew about the organization to a certain media outlet. Luckily, that media outlet was already in Gable's pocket. Gable used them to test trainees for loyalty because loyalty meant everything. It was one of the reasons that the Desire Card had prospered for almost forty years of business.

J.D. wasn't a part of the mission to oust Spencer Tracy, but he heard whispers of what went down. Tracy had gotten wind of a coup and fled to the upper reaches of Finland, a shade away from the Arctic, thinking he'd be safe. But he was sloppy and told his tale to one too many Finns. He also chose a ridiculous alias of Tracy Spencer as if no one would make the connection. Marlon Brando and Fred Astaire caught up with him in the city of Oulu, dragged him out into the wilderness and buried him alive under an ice fishing pond. Sometime last spring, Spencer Tracy finally floated to the surface, his face peeled off and frozen next to him. That was what happened to snitches. Who knew what might be in store for a deserter?

But as Marcus Edmonton, he won't make those

same errors. Besides Annie, no one will ever know his true identity again. He'll follow along with whatever scheme her sleazy boyfriend is planning so he can get a gun and enough cash to fly to Fiji. He won't fail because failure means his head on a plate. Once he reaches paradise, he'll nab some simple job and lay low, eventually find a local woman to love and have a kid or two, be completely normal, blissfully normal, and nothing more. He'll take pleasure in the beauty of sunsets and look toward his future rather than his past.

But for now, that's just a pipe dream, so he can't let himself think about it anymore while he's still in Killenroy.

Gun. Cash. *Adios.*

Then he can get ready to embrace paradise.

## 22

Trigger Happy hasn't changed a lick in eight long years. Still with a red neon sign of a gun shooting its name above the door, still full of tough types warming the stools around a horseshoe-shaped bar. The dark and grubby place clogged with cigarette smoke and a mix of truckers, loggers, and leave-me-the-hell-alone loners.

Annie's near a booth in the back surrounded by a group of four guys.

The two who catch J.D.'s eye first are a pair of giant muscled twins, identical except Twin #1 has a shaved scalp and Twin #2 has longer hair. Their heads are the size of medicine balls, their necks as thick as his waist with forearms that look like thighs. He's never trusted anyone with the ability to crush someone one-handed. Already they're eyeing him back: swigging beers from the side of their mouths, grunting nonsensically to each other, planning his takedown if necessary.

In between them stands their opposite, a small and wiry guy no more than a buck ten. He has big eyes peering from coke-bottle glasses and a nervous twitch, his voice hovering around a falsetto tone that J.D. can hear from yards away.

None of them seem like Annie's type so J.D. pegs the fourth guy as her beau. Dirty blond hair that a girl might dub strawberry blond. A scruffy beard and a mean smirk. The guy spits a brownish substance into an empty beer bottle and then wipes his mouth with the back of his hand. J.D. spies two suspect tattoos: the number 88 on his bicep and a spider web on his elbow, symbols of White Power and time spent in prison.

Annie finally notices J.D. at the door and waves him over.

"Marcus, you made it."

*Attagirl.* Annie's a pro who wouldn't get tripped up over an alias.

"Abram, this is the guy I was telling you about. The ex-soldier."

"Marcus Edmonton," J.D. says, extending his hand.

Abram looks him up and down and spits another loogie into his beer bottle before shaking J.D.'s hand.

"And you were a sniper?"

"Until I got stabbed in the eye."

"Fuckin' Dune Coon got ya, didn't they?"

The rest of the crew murmurs some other racial slurs.

"I swear I'm as sharp a shot as ever," J.D. says. "The Army may have thought the injury affected my depth perception, but it hasn't."

"I'll have to see with my own two eyes how good you still are," Abram says, snorting through his nose. "My own *two* eyes...ha! I kill me."

"Abram, you don't have to be mean about it," Annie says.

"Hell, Marcus knows I'm kidding, that's what I do. Right, boys?"

Each of the crew agrees that Abram's a kidder, the hierarchy of the gang instantly revealed. Abram's the boss and the rest of them are his yes-men. The fact that the two enormous Twins fall in line with whatever he says automatically means they can't be too bright.

"So Annie told me you guys used to know each other?" Abram asks, his hand on J.D.'s shoulder.

"We did, some years ago."

Abram spits another loogie into his bottle, thick and viscous like molasses.

"She said she ran into you outside the Border Diner yesterday morning?"

It's hard to tell whether Abram is fishing for lies, or if he's just making small talk. Can he smell Annie's deceit? Did her place still reek of sex when the guy returned from Canada?

"Yeah, we ran into each other yesterday," J.D. says, with a gracious, good-guy grin. "I was hitchhiking through this area. Looking for work."

"What kind of work?"

"Whatever pays and pays fast. Willing to do anything."

"Anything, huh? Well, okay."

Abram indicates the two giant muscle guys book-ending him. "These here are the Twins."

Both Twins nod in sync.

"They don't say much. But muscle doesn't really need to say much. You can just call 'em Dumb and Dumber."

He points to the wiry guy who's fidgeting in place. "Over there's Peanut."

Peanut gives a nervous wave.

"Peanut's smart as shit, but he's got the strength of a twelve-year-old girl."

Abram gets Peanut in a headlock, nearly flips the guy over. He has a manic energy that's definitely drug fueled. Coke? Meth? Possibly a cocktail of the two. J.D. knows the downside of dealing with druggies is that they're unreliable, but the upside is they're easy to bamboozle.

"C'mon, Abram, c'mon," Peanut whines, his face turning a bright pink.

Abram loses interest and pushes Peanut away. He turns to Annie.

"Babe, go get us some more brews and leave us boys to talk."

He slaps Annie's butt before sending her off towards the bar. He leans in close to J.D.

"Girl is a freak in the sheets—anything goes. You ever tap that?"

J.D. shakes his head.

"Good looking Army stud like you never had that snatch? Tastes like a glazed donut down there."

He flings his arm around J.D. and leads him over to a booth. The Twins and Peanut follow.

"Now I was just telling my boys about a job coming our very way. Mucho, mucho *di-ne-ro*."

"I'm interested."

"Fuck yeah, you're interested. You ever shot a man other than some Q-Tip Head?"

"I've shot...a few."

"I bet you have. You a stone-cold motherfucker, I can tell."

"I need a fake passport," J.D. says, getting right down to business. "You able to make that happen?"

"Peanut's got that covered, he's good for that."

"Yeah, easy peasy," Peanut declares, still rubbing his sore neck.

"Easy peasy, what the fuck does that even mean? I swear, sometimes you're nothing more than one of those retarded dolls with a string. Now shut up while I explain the plan to Marcus over here."

Peanut sinks down in his seat.

Abram gives a brotherly nod to J.D. to show that he's above the rest of his crew, the loyal soldiers that he controls. It's a look that J.D. knows all too well, one he often saw reflected behind Gable's mask.

There isn't a boss out there that doesn't like to swing his dick around, J.D. thinks; but Abram's not a threat in the least, just a small-time thug who's come into his life for a reason. Should this 'plan' sound worthwhile, it's the best chance he's got right now for a shot at survival.

It may even be the only shot he'll get.

# 23

"So, I'm in a bar across the border yesterday," Abram says, rubbing his hands together as he begins his tale. "Real dumpster I found with the beer tasting like they put old sweat socks in the tap. In the booth behind me are these two goons having a conversation about something big going down. From the looks of it, they've had one too many and become a little loose-lipped. Talking about shipping kilos of coke across the border in a van. Aiming to unload it in Junction, that's the next town over."

A smile breaks out on Abram's greedy face.

"They're getting a massive deal for the blow in Canada and want to sell it here where it'll be cut with baking soda and they can jack up the price. Say they've got some contact here who'll help them move it. They've also got a friend working border patrol so they figure it's a done deal."

"Cutting it with baking soda won't work," J.D. interrupts. "People will be able to tell."

"Exactly. Which shows that these guys ain't too

swift. Anyway, every town 'round these parts is broker than broke. So my idea is we steal their blow and sell it off to one buyer bigger than this area. Easy peas... Peanut, what was that dumb phrase again?"

"Easy peasy lemon squeezy. It comes from a 70s detergent commercial where a little girl proves to her mom how easy the detergent cleans–"

Abram gives Peanut a dirty look. *Shut the fuck up again, Peanut.*

"You have a buyer already?" J.D. asks.

Abram fires a pretend gun at J.D., nods his head.

"You ask all the right questions, stranger. Yeah, I got someone in mind. Calls himself The Doctor."

The name evokes a response in each of the crew. The Twins gulp simultaneously while Peanut starts picking at the dirt under his fingernails.

"Everyone in these parts knows about The Doctor," Abram continues. "Bit of an urban legend."

"He killed someone's dog once after an owed payment came too late," Peanut says, digging deeper into a pesky fingernail.

"He cut off an employee's lips after the guy threatened to tell the cops about his operation," Twin #1 adds.

"That make you scared, Twin?" Abram asks.

"I'm just sayin'," says Twin #1.

"Anyhoo, we just have to convince The Doctor that we can intercept the drugs. Then we'll sell it to him for an unbeatable price."

"Have you worked with this Doctor before?"

"Sure have. He's a nasty son-of-a-b, but a man of his word."

Abram goes to take a swill of his beer and realizes it's full of loogies. He tosses it aside.

"This sound like somethin' you'd be into, Marcus? We don't plan on gunning down these goons, but we need a crack shot just in case there's trouble."

"Could you get me a gun as soon as possible?"

"The goons are coming through two days from now," Abram says. "I can get ya a CZ 75B by then. How's that sound?"

Honestly not ideal, J.D. wants to admit, but what better choice does he have? That means two days of being extra on guard with the Kamikaze Knife ready to go in his waistband.

"Of course, I want to line up some cans first and see how good a shot you really are," Abram says. "Whether that missing eye of yours might be a problem?"

Ah, cans. J.D.'s old friends from when he was just a squirt. He knows his talent will blow them all away, but he can't help but wonder how Gramps would feel about his hunting lessons being put to this kind of use. None too happy, he surmises, except Gramps always billed himself as a survivalist. We fall into dicey situations and have to claw our way out any way we can. That's the way the world works. Whatever moral boundaries may have been crossed over the years, Gramps would still want him to survive at all costs. He'd demand it.

Annie returns with five bottles of beer between her fingers. She places them on the booth.

"Thanks, hon," Abram says, groping her in his disgusting way as he pulls her in for a kiss. She sits down.

"So, Marcus, Abram do his number on you?" Annie asks. "He could sell wood to a forest."

J.D. leans back and picks at the label on his beer. He weighs the percentages of this scheme working out —none too good, he imagines, but at least he'll have a gun and a fake passport by the end of it. There's no other scenario he can think of that would get him both this fast. If the money happens as well, he'll chalk that up to a bonus. If not, he'll head to the next town and hope his goldmine might be there.

"I'm in," he says, cracking his knuckles. "Let's go shoot some cans and meet this Doctor."

## 24

An afternoon of shooting cans, the crew gaping at J.D.'s skill. Not a can left standing by the end of it, even when Abram makes him aim from the farthest distance possible. As a sniper, he'd been expected to hit targets from half a mile away, so all of Abram's requests are cake. Afterwards they hop in a pickup to head to The Doctor's. Abram's at the wheel, J.D. in shotgun, Peanut squeezing between the two, and the Twins in the back causing the truck to feel bottom heavy.

"The Doctor's been the go-to guy for blow in these parts for years," Abram says, one hand on the wheel, the other ripping at a funky smelling (and looking) cigarette. "He farms it out through the Northwest. Hires underlings to work in-house. Requires them all to be nude so they won't pocket his shit. And he's not afraid to rough anyone up if he thinks they're scamming him. Likens himself to an old-time gangster like Frank Lucas or something."

"How big is the operation?" J.D. asks.

"Pretty massive. The Doctor's well connected so he'll be able to unload whatever we get him in a blink. That's why he'll pay good for it."

Peanut has switched from digging the dirt out of his fingernails to gnawing at them.

"Peanut, you want to be less nasty for once?" Abram says, slapping him on the back of his head.

"Sorry, The Doctor just makes me nervous."

"Pissing makes you nervous."

"Why do they call him The Doctor?" J.D. asks.

"They say he once was an actual doctor decades ago, but lost his license after a large malpractice suit. Found himself a more lucrative profession."

The pick-up truck heads off the main road down a dirt path through a forest. The sounds of traffic becoming muted. They turn onto an even narrower path past all signs of civilization. This is where people go to die, J.D. thinks. No one around to hear the screams.

"Here we are," Abram says, as they pull up to an aquamarine-colored shack, the front windows boarded up with wood slats.

The crew steps out and Abram knocks on the door.

"Who the fuck is it?" a deep voice asks from inside.

"It's Abram, man. I told The Doctor I'd be stopping by."

They hear murmuring from inside.

The door opens to two large Black guards packing serious heat. They wave Abram and J.D. in, but stop the rest of the crew.

"This ain't no party," one of the guards says. "Pip-squeak and the two skyscrapers are gonna have to wait outside."

The Twins aren't pleased, but Abram nods for them to be cool.

They enter the shack and the guards shut the door. Music pumps in the background. The Doctor is sitting on a lounge chair with a high back like a throne. Tall and thin, he wears purple John Lennon sunglasses and has his stringy graying hair in a ponytail. He's got liver spots galore and a leathery suitcase kind-of-tan. He radiates a certain presence, an ominous aura that reminds J.D. of Gable, someone who's been responsible for causing a lot of death. He's only recognized this in a few men before.

Surrounding The Doctor is his enterprise: scales, giant bags of coke, bill-counting machines. A bevy of young naked men and women swish around the place cutting up the coke, weighing it, and counting the cash.

The Doctor grabs a guy with slick hair by the arm as he passes by. He pulls him down to his level to inspect his nose. Traces of white powder linger. He slaps him hard across the face and then takes a bump from a silver tray at his side. The guy scoots away, licking the inside of his throbbing cheek.

Abram scurries over like a lapdog.

"Ah, the magnificent Doctor," he says. "It sure has been a while. You are look-ing good, my brother."

The Doctor raises an eyebrow, already annoyed by Abram.

"Tell me about this deal of a lifetime and save the ass kissing for someone who gives a rat's fuck," The Doctor says, his voice sounding like he's been gargling with glass.

Abram becomes tongue-tied, reorganizes his pitch.

"Uh...so primo stuff coming into Junction. Kilos of candy cane."

"I'm listening," The Doctor says, raising his other eyebrow.

"Two-bit crooks are doing a run through these parts without a fucking clue between them. Easy peasy to swipe, and we'll sell it solely to you for a bargain."

The Doctor dips his finger into a pile of coke and runs it across his teeth. He smiles a bleeding-gums smile and glances at J.D.

"Why's One Eye over here looking at me funny?"

"This is my new partner Marcus. He's here to make sure–"

The Doctor holds his hand up. "I don't give a cat's piss about any new partners you have or the particulars of your scheme. You produce the goods and we'll talk."

He bids them both away.

"You got it, Doctor. Certainly. We'll show ourselves out...."

The Doctor picks up a remote and turns on some music until Abram's voice is drowned out. "Take On Me," by A-Ha.

The Doctor gestures for the guy with slick hair to come over. He's talking to him very sternly.

Abram yanks at J.D. to leave.

The guy with the slick hair turns his face towards them, the right side swollen and purple. A look of fear like a windstorm in his eyes. Enough to warn J.D. that there's no way this brand-new alliance will end well.

# 25

BACK AT THE BEDBUG, J.D. WAKES FROM A FITFUL dream in the middle of the night. The sheets are soaked. For a second he thinks its blood. He's fully dressed, the knife on the bedside table easily in reach. The sound of the door creaking open. The room drenched in darkness except for one band of moonlight passing through the curtains. His left eye zeroing in on a shadow. The click of the door as it closes. The shadow growing in length along the wall, its steps barely audible. Somehow, he's become paralyzed, unable to reach for the knife. Was he given an injection of something, or is it just fear keeping him glued to the bed? Fear because he can recognize the shadow once the moonlight reveals its face.

Gable in the flesh. Slicked-back hair and a mustache that doesn't give a damn.

"My slippery soldier," Gable whispers, the robotic pitch of his voice lower than ever. "Haven't you realized that no one ever crosses me and lives to tell the story?"

J.D. glances at the knife. It's inches away but it might as well be a mile.

"Not so fast, Dean."

*It's Storm.*

J.D.'s only able to think this, but it's written all over his face. He wants Gable to understand that refusing to lose his soul anymore means a shred of it remains, even if this winds up being the end for him.

"You know you were one of my best," Gable says, taking out an FNP 45 handgun with a silencer, pointing it square at J.D.'s forehead. Stainless steel construction, front and rear cocking serrations, slide cut and threading for optional electronic red-dot sight.

"Every decade an operative like you comes around, Dean. Someone who's always gotten the target in one shot. Who can slip in and out of their mask at the precise time so they'll never get caught. Who never leaves a trace of evidence behind. Who is Clean. Collected. Remorseless. That was how I found you. Broken and uninterested in piecing yourself back together. And you loved it. Every second of it. The power. The pull of the trigger. The rush of it all."

"Something...changed," J.D.'s able to murmur, which means that whatever he's been drugged with is starting to wear off.

"Souls don't grow back," Gable says, his robotic pitch getting angrier. "We are all headed to hell in the same boat."

"There is a special...type of hell...waiting for you... and you alone."

"You truly believe that?" Gable chuckles. "That we are a different kind of evil? I've never had an actual drop of someone's blood on my hands. You, my soldier, are up to your elbows."

J.D. hears the click of the safety disengaging.

Suddenly he feels a twinge of movement in his thumb. Then his index finger wiggles and the rest of his hand follows suit. If he can stall for time, he's got a shot at the knife.

"Who are you?" J.D. gasps. "Under your mask? At least let me see. I don't believe you have a face."

He can clench his fingers now, a tingle slowly spreading up his palm.

"I'm someone you'd least expect."

Gable begins to peel off his mask.

For a moment, J.D. forgets about the knife, too caught up in the fascination of Gable's true identity, of seven years of speculation finally put to rest. Is the Boss scarred just like the rest of them? Is his face a map of his pain? Is that why he needs to torture so many?

A burning sensation spreads through J.D.'s heart as the mask is tossed to the side.

Staring back is The Doctor with a bleeding gums smile.

"What...the fuck...?"

"I have a diagnosis for you," The Doctor says, his tongue flicking over his bloodstained teeth. "This scam of yours will not work and there won't be a ticket to paradise in your future. Nothing can save you now."

A surge of life shoots up J.D.'s arm. He cries out and uses all his might to reach for the knife. He grabs the handle just as The Doctor pulls the trigger. The last sound he hears is a mocking laugh that gets cut off in mid-cackle.

And then darkness. So much darkness.

## 26

J.D. SHOOTS OUT OF BED IN A COLD SWEAT, REELING from having a nightmare within a dream. The image of Gable and The Doctor coalescing into one malevolent being remains locked in his skull. So does the experience of witnessing his own death. He wonders if it was all a prophecy. Has he brought a whole new world of trouble to his feet by associating with another proven psychopath, or will one evil actually save him from the other?

No time to worry about that now. Outside the door, he can hear footsteps. There's a possibility that this could be another dream, some never-ending continuum he's entered, but he can't take the chance. He grabs the Kamikaze Knife from under the mattress, leaps off the bed, and flings open the door ready to stab.

Annie stands there in shock.

"Annie? What the...?"

She's visibly upset, her face stained with tears.

"J.D., I didn't know where else to go."

He lowers the knife in a daze. Peers down the

hallway for a sign of the enemy. He pulls her inside and shuts the door.

"How did you know my room number?"

"It's not too hard to find the guy with an eye patch," she says, her finger running under her nose. "Lady at the front desk remembered you well."

"I should switch rooms," he says, as he sticks the knife back under the mattress. And then quietly to himself: "And lose the eye patch."

"Listen, I know it's real late and all, but Abram and I had a fight." She winces as she rubs her collarbone. "The bastard hit me."

He's unsure of what to do or say. Part of him wants to embrace her, to vow to make Abram pay, to get her far away from Killenroy; but he's frozen just like in his dream.

"Abram's just nervous about working with The Doctor, that's all," Annie says, sounding like she doesn't even believe her own excuse.

"So am I, but I'd never hit you."

"I know. You're one of the truly good ones."

"You're not thinking about going back to him, are you?"

"Abram won't do it again, and besides he didn't touch my face. He never touches my face."

"You're a fool."

She nods, sways in place.

"That's what my new friend Carmen says. After Abram beat on me, I went to Trigger Happy and met her. This town is three-to-one guys-to-girls so girlfriends are hard to come by. Anyway, Carmen came from an abusive relationship too. Isn't that funny? My Mama would've said 'that's God bringin' people together.'"

"Or the Devil."

"Abram's not that bad. There's worse than him. He's just weak. I'm letting you know this since you'll be going into business with him."

"I know exactly the kind of man I'm getting into business with."

"Carmen's staying at the Bedbug too. After I walked her back, I found myself just thinkin' about you."

She unclasps the belt cinching her coat and reveals a baby blue negligee.

"I've been thinkin' 'bout you a lot, J.D. About last night. About our week together so many years ago."

He's been thinking about her too, a reprieve from the paranoia, just a taste. He deserves that taste.

"Offer still stand for another go-round?" she asks, removing her coat and letting the negligee slide to the floor. She's completely naked except for a pair of worn cowboy boots.

He touches the bruise on her collarbone, purple and swollen in the glare of the moonlight. He kisses it. Kisses her.

———

While making love to Annie, J.D. makes sure to keep his good eye open the entire time. He wants to burn the image of this night into his brain, since he knows their relationship is too doomed to ever work out. At one point, she takes off his eye patch and pulls him deeper inside of her, caresses his eye socket with her tongue. Briefly, he thinks he can sense a pulse in his optic nerve, but then they come together and he focuses on holding her close instead, tight enough to feel her heartbeat against his palm.

She laughs as she finally kicks off her cowboy boots.

"You didn't even give me a chance to lose 'em," she says, tucking a blond strand of her hair around her ear.

"I'm impatient."

"No, J.D., you're very patient. And careful. And considerate. The way you touch me makes me feel like I'm the only girl in the world. Abram's all, 'C'mon, did you come yet or what?'"

"Why are you with him then?"

"I'm sorry, I didn't mean to bring Abram up. I don't want to talk no more about him. Let's only talk about good things. I want to hear about this paradise you'll be heading to."

He blinks and she's there with him: beaches without another soul around, coconut trees towering to the sky, the water as clear as glass. What if he took her with him? Since the Card is looking for someone who's traveling solo, Annie could be the camouflage he needs. But can he trust her with the secret of that paradise? Can he trust anyone?

"There's this place called Matagi Island," he says, the words unraveling from his mouth without any effort to stop them. "Used to be a volcano, but the crater fell away on one side and now it's a white sand beach. That's where I want to go."

She traces a finger around his nipple.

"You know we can't do this again, J.D."

He sighs, a deep one that's been weeks in the making.

"I know."

"You'll be leaving soon once the job is done, and if Abram found out about us..."

"Do you want me to ask you to come along?"

She stops rubbing his chest.

"You mean to this island?"

"It's in Fiji," he says, trying to gauge what she's thinking. Over the years he's honed his ability to read people's minds, but she's a blank slate.

"We both know that ain't likely," she finally says, looking away after a moment. "I'll never leave this place."

"What's keeping you here?"

"I've given up. I'm not good no more. I haven't been in a while. Somewhere like Killenroy is all that'll have me."

"What about your family?"

"Go back to Kentucky? They know my past, the bad things I've done. They're Bible thumpers and I'm a heathen who doesn't exist."

"I've done some bad things too, truly bad things, things that I regret. But who's to say that's who we have to be anymore?"

She glances at the hovering moon, as if considering. A tear trickles from her eye.

"It's too late. All those bad things have made us who we are. We gotta pay for our rotten choices, and I'll be paying for the rest of my life in a purgatory called Killenroy."

"Why punish yourself like that?"

"Cause I'm still capable of doing bad things. It's in me, wrestling around, always will be."

He strokes her cheek, wipes away the lone tear.

"I don't care. Come with me. Matagi Island. I mean it, Annie."

She manages a tiny smile.

"Just for tonight, J.D., let's pretend I said yes."

She's staring at the gaping hole where his right eye used to be.

"You know, you should lose the eye patch for good."

"It doesn't weird you out?"

"Everyone has scars," she says, her fingers gliding over her purpling collarbone. "Why hide them?"

He thinks of all the operatives at the Card with their masks and mutilated faces, trading their souls for a chance to appear normal.

"You're right," he says, picking up the eye patch on the bedside table and tossing it in the garbage can. He leans in closer so she could caress his socket again.

This time, he swears he can feel the sensation of her touch.

## 27

AT TRIGGER HAPPY THE NEXT DAY, J.D.'S HUNCHED around a booth in the back with Abram, Peanut, and the Twins. Empty beer bottles and overloaded ashtrays abound. Bad country music coming from the juke. A waitress with long hair down to her butt comes by to collect the empties. Abram waves her away as he begins to tell the crew about The Plan.

"So there's this stoplight that the Goons will have to pass on the way to Junction."

Abram pauses to suck at a cigarette that's already been smoked down to the filter. He's got an animated energy about him, definitely drug fueled. The words exploding from his mouth in a frenzy.

"Ain't no way these Goons can get into Junction otherwise. Problem is that we've got no idea what time they're arriving, so we'll have to wait at the stoplight starting at the crack of dawn."

"How will we recognize their van?" Peanut asks.

"We look for one with Canadian plates, dipshit." Abram stabs his cigarette butt on top of a mountain of others. He takes out a toothpick from his front pocket and pops it in his mouth instead. "The instant we see a motherfuckin' red leaf, the Twins'll jump out and put the fear in them at the light."

The Twins perk up at the mention of their name.

"You both shoot 'em unless they let you in their van. You hear that, #1 and #2? You be ready to put a bullet in their goddamn skulls if they don't let you inside."

"Okay, then what?" J.D. asks, wanting to move this along and hear his part in the scheme.

Abram gives J.D. a look. *Know your place, grunt,* his eyes say. *This is my rodeo.*

"So once the Twins are in the van, they'll make the Goons head deep into the woods. The three of us will follow in my truck. Then we'll rob their stash and head to The Doctor. Then we'll go back to Annie's and split up the cash."

He points at J.D. with his toothpick.

"You're there in case anything goes sour and someone needs to be taken care of. Ideally, I only wanna knock these guys unconscious. I'm not planning to kill anyone, but things don't always go as planned."

"No they don't," J.D. says.

"There's something different about you today, Marcus."

The rest of the crew agrees with this assessment.

J.D. can feel an imaginary spider crawling down the back of his neck. Does Abram know that Annie stayed over at the Bedbug last night? That the two of them fucked till the sun rose? He wonders if he's been sitting at the booth with a dopey grin on his face this whole time.

"I know what it is," Abram says, as if he's realized

some mystical revelation. "You ain't got no eye patch anymore."

"Oh yeah...just wasn't comfortable."

"You might think about putting it back on. That eye socket of yours looks like a midget's gnarly vagina."

Abram lets out a rapid-fire laugh and the crew joins in.

J.D. wants to bash Abram's face into the overflowing ashtray, to wedge every last cigarette butt into the guy's right eye until it falls out. You never hit a woman. Who could ever want to cause Annie pain? He knows he'll need to get retribution for her bruises before he leaves town. He'll have to make sure that Abram won't be laughing again for some time.

"Midget's vagina," Abram whistles, wiping the tears from his eyes. "I do slay me."

The front door swings open and Annie enters with a red-haired woman at her side. As she walks over to the booth, time slows down for J.D. He's been zapped inside a music video, the juke playing a sappy country love song that becomes a soundtrack to Annie's steps.

"Hey fellas, this is my girlfriend Carmen," she says.

Carmen appears plastic, nothing compared to Annie. She's young but has had too much work done to her face. Nipped and tucked until she's barely real anymore.

"Boys, this round is on me," Carmen says. "I'll be right back."

Abram makes a show of ogling her as she walks away.

"Abram..." Annie says, shaking her head.

"Baby, ain't no harm in looking." He high-fives Twin #2.

Annie touches J.D.'s shoulder, her hand lingering for an extra moment. "Hi, Marcus."

"Annie," he nods back.

Abram's finished high-fiving the rest of the crew. He raises his palm for J.D. to reciprocate, but he's got his eye on his girl. He must know something's been going on.

J.D. high-fives Abram back, thinking that both of them probably want to kill each other at this moment for different reasons.

# 28

THE JUKEBOX HAS SWITCHED TO ROCK MUSIC, A sleazy number with a pumping baseline and a heavy use of wah-wah, a more fitting tribute to the plan they've all cooked up. Abram's visibly upset with Annie over in the corner. J.D. is at the booth with the rest of the crew and Carmen, trying to drown out their bullshit ramblings so he can focus on the lover's spat. From his training, he's learned how to hone his ear well.

"You're always picking up strays," he can hear Abram saying.

"No, Abram, it's not like that."

J.D. shifts in his seat so he could grab the knife in his waistband if Abram decides to start something and attack him. He'd have to go for the Twins first, quick stabs to their throats so they'd no longer be a threat. Then he'd get Abram in the belly. It's hard to tell how Annie would react. If she'd stand by her man, or spit on his corpse.

"She's just a friend of mine," Annie says, and

instantly J.D. can relax. They're only talking about Carmen.

"Someday one of these strays is gonna bite you in the ass, Annie. You didn't tell her about the job we're planning, did you?"

"You never tell me nothin' anyway. Just to wait at home for y'all to come over when it's done. And that it involves drugs."

"Will you shut–You can't just trust random people like that, don't you get it? Not with the kind of work we do."

"You think she's a cop? C'mon, Abram, I need more girlfriends. It's not healthy for me to just be around you and the Three Stooges."

"I'm taking you home."

He grabs her arm but she doesn't budge. He twists her wrist hard enough to make her yelp.

J.D. reaches for his knife again, ready to pounce on Abram should it escalate, but Annie manages to pull herself away.

"I can go by myself, jackass." She bashes into Abram's shoulder on her way towards the door. "Don't follow me, Abram. You hear? You stay away!"

She's yelling loud enough to be heard over the rock music. All the regulars turn around to watch. She caters to the audience by fixing her hair and stomping out of the bar.

Abram shrugs his shoulders and joins the rest of them at the booth.

"Is Annie okay?" Peanut asks.

"Is that girl ever okay?" Abram says, clapping his hands. "Let's go, boys, we need to be fresh for tomorrow."

The Twins and Peanut get up. J.D. stands as well, but Carmen places her hand on his.

"I haven't finished my drink yet," she says, as if that's his fault. "Don't leave me all alone."

Abram squeezes J.D.'s shoulder and pushes him down in his seat.

"A beautiful lady has made a request, Marcus. I believe you have to do what she says. We'll pick you up at your motel come dawn."

Peanut takes out a camera and snaps a picture, the flash blinding.

"For your new passport photo," he says.

J.D. blinks until he can see straight again, then gives a thumbs up.

Abram leans in closer, his breath reeking of booze. J.D. figures he's about to get some kind of threatening warning about staying away from Annie. He's surprised when Abram just raises his eyebrows at Carmen.

"Let me know if the carpet's red, too."

Abram makes a sexual gesture with his fingers and then staggers out of the bar. The rest of the crew drunkenly follows.

Carmen lights a long cigarette, her lips injected and huge, a living doll brought to life.

"You've known these guys long?" she asks.

J.D. finally lets go of the knife's handle, his fingers throbbing from the intensity of the last few minutes.

"I've known them long enough."

"Annie says you're all working on a job together."

She taps her fake nose with a smile. "Drug heist," she whispers.

His good eye watches her closely. What's her angle? Everyone's always got an angle.

"Annie told you that?"

"Yeah, we got real close, real fast. Similar problems with men. My ex messed up my face pretty bad. But a few reconstructive surgeries and I'm all better."

He doesn't say anything. He's caught up in picturing Annie divulging her entire sad story at the bar last night, her collarbone all black and blue.

"This is when you tell me my face looks good," Carmen says, offended.

He has no time to deal with a distraction like her. He's only staying in his seat so he doesn't make a stupid move and go after Annie. The most important thing is to mentally prepare for tomorrow. A good night's sleep should be all that's in the cards for tonight.

"It looks good," he eventually says to appease, but it doesn't sound convincing.

"It looks like something I guess. Not quite human anymore, but I'm okay with that." She nods at his eye. "Ever thought about getting a fake one that looks real?"

"I'm still human," he says, the thought appearing out of nowhere.

Carmen places her hand over his again.

"I'm sorry, I didn't mean to offend. I don't meet too many people who can relate in any way."

She widens her eyes, but there's no sign of life in them.

"So tell me more about this drug heist. Maybe I could help?"

There's the angle, just like he figured. He's done with entertaining her, and since he's convinced he's not gonna go after Annie anymore, he chugs the rest of his beer and gets up to leave.

"Wait a minute," Carmen says, more forceful than

before. Now there's something behind her eyes, she's hungry. "Annie said there might be a way for me to get involved."

"I'm not the one to ask."

"So it's her boyfriend Abram that runs the whole show? Everyone does whatever he says. He's the boss and you're just his lackey?"

J.D. slams his fist on the table. "He's not the boss of me, no one is the boss of me."

He's twisted his body now so the knife is exposed. Carmen catches sight of it and starts breathing heavier.

"Fuck," he says, fixing his shirt so the knife becomes hidden again. "I'm sorry, I...have a lot on my mind. I need to go."

"I'm staying at the same motel," she says, getting up as well, stuck at his side. He practically has to shake her off. "I can walk you back. I'm really good at helping someone relax...if you give me a chance."

"Yeah, no thanks."

She slips back into the booth; her face looking like it's struggling to hang on. She roots in her purse and whips out another cigarette to ease her mourning, but he doesn't care. He's already gone.

# 29

J.D. SLEPT THAT NIGHT LIKE HE WAS LYING IN A coffin, hands crossed over his chest, kamikaze knife at his side. When he got back from Trigger Happy, he had the woman behind the desk switch his room, made her promise under no circumstance to tell any visitors the number. Even if Annie tried to come by, he didn't want to see her, at least not until the cash and a gun were in his hands.

Then he could figure out his next step and whether she'll be a part of it.

———

Before dawn breaks, he hears a car horn sounding from the parking lot. He peeks outside the window to see the two giant Twins wedged in the back of a pick-up, while Abram and Peanut have a smoke up front. Abram's leaning on the car horn, drawing too much attention already.

By the mirror above the bureau, he fishes in the

garbage can and puts his eye patch back on. He'll wear it just until the job is finished, then he'll lose it for good. He places the knife back in his waistband and slips out the door as the car horn continues to wake up the entire motel.

———

Minutes later, J.D. is waiting at the cross street of Burre and Lansing with the stoplight in view. The Twins are around the corner out of sight, a walkie-talkie connecting them to Abram at the wheel. Peanut's been relegated to the back. Peanut hands over J.D.'s new fake passport. In the picture, J.D. looks surprised, as if he has no idea what he's posing for. Next Peanut passes him a CZ 75B, the gun he's been waiting for, featuring a staggered-column magazine, all-steel construction, and a hammer-forged barrel. This one's a second generation with an internal firing pin safety and a squared and serrated trigger guard too. J.D. practically wants to cry. He lets out a huge breath of relief, unable to do so since Bud took his 9mm away.

The sun winks along the horizon, slowly rising upward. Not a car in sight yet. The town even more forlorn during the early hours, void of people. J.D. figures that all the meth heads like to sleep in.

Abram snorts a thimble-full of coke, rubs his hands together, motions for J.D. to join him but J.D. declines. They hear a rumbling sound behind them, tires creeping against asphalt. A white van pulls up to the stoplight. Too dark outside to see inside the windows as it passes, but J.D.'s stomach lurches.

"Lookie, lookie here," Abram says.

The van's license plate comes in view. Washington State.

"No dice yet," Abram says, taking his second bump of the day. "Say, you get lucky with that sweet piece of red last night?"

His bloodshot eyes linger over J.D.

"She's not really my type."

Abram chews on his lip, drums the steering wheel.

"And what would that type be, Marcus? Cause my type is twat, don't really care what's attached to it."

"I guess I do care."

Abram passes over the thimble of coke.

"No, I'm good, man."

"Brother, we're about to pull off something spectacular. Let's get your blood flowing."

He punches J.D. in the arm, practically sticks the thimble under J.D.'s nose.

J.D. takes the thimble, even though there's no way in hell he's gonna snort it and risk losing a shred of focus. That might just be what Abram wants.

"You know, Annie didn't come over to my place last night like she usually does," says Abram, a hint of aggression in his voice. "You didn't happen to see her, did you?"

"I spent the night alone."

"Yeah, I bet you did."

Since J.D. hasn't seen Annie since Trigger Happy, he's got nothing to hide. Still, he clutches the CZ 75B, not trusting a batshit crazy fuck like Abram for a second.

They hear the sound of wheels coming from down the road again. Abram spins around, long enough for J.D. to toss the coke out of the window.

"Good stuff," he says, rubbing his nose once Abram looks back.

Through the rear-view, he can tell that Peanut was watching him; but the guy doesn't say anything to Abram, just shoves a bunch of fingers in his mouth.

Still, he'll have to keep his eye on Peanut as well. He knows that usually the quiet ones can wind up causing the most trouble.

# 30

By late afternoon, three vans have passed through the stoplight but none with Canadian plates. J.D. has counted the seconds before it turns from red to green, just under a minute. Might be tough for two ogres like the Twins to get there in time, however Abram doesn't seem to be worried.

"The Twins are beasts," Abram says, "they may each weigh a ton but they're quick as fuck."

He goes into a rant about how the whole crew ultimately met because of a guy name Gooch (RIP) who headed up a gun running gang in Wenatchee. Gooch got pegged by the Feds, turned state's evidence for a shorter sentence, but then took a life-changing shower in prison when a former member named Yahtzee slit his throat. Abram was in for a bank heist at the time, Twin #1 in for arson. Both of them saved their own asses by holding Gooch down while psychotic Yahtzee whipped out a razorblade. Yahtzee got the chair eventually, but Abram and Twin #1 had bonded. They wound up being released around the same time and headed back to Killenroy together to make some fast cash. Twin #1 soon got his brother to join and Abram contacted his ol' buddy Peanut from high school who'd been hanging around not doing much of anything. Their first scam was a home robbery in Everett, a neighbor of Twin #2's who had announced his impending vacation and kept tons of cash in his house since he didn't trust banks. The robbery was sweet and easy enough to solidify the crew as a force to be reckoned with. Fast forward to three years later and now they're possibly on the heels of their biggest take-home yet.

"I trust them more than I trust my own blood," Abram says, still animated from his frequent toots throughout the day; but J.D. doesn't have a chance to respond. In the distance, he can see a black van approaching through the side mirror.

The van pulls up to the stoplight. Sure enough, Canadian plates.

"Show time," Abram says, into the walkie-talkie.

"Copy that," one of the Twins responds.

Everyone puts a pantyhose leg over their face.

The Twins emerge from around the corner with their faces covered too. They split from one another and point their guns at both sides of the van. They're yelling for the driver to open the door, ready to fire.

The light changes to green, the van about to take off.

Twin #1 bashes the handle of his gun into the window. Glass shatters. He reaches inside and sticks the barrel of the gun into the driver's nose.

Finally, the van's door opens and the Twins hop inside. It slowly rolls down the street as Abram puts the pick-up in drive and follows.

The sun is setting now, shriveling into the far away mountains. They pursue the black van through twisty roads until it turns down a path leading towards the woods. Tall and thin trees all on top of one another. They drive until the road they came in on is no longer in sight.

At a clearing, the black van stops and the Twins force the Goons outside. Abram leaps out as well, J.D. and Peanut close behind. A chorus of cicadas rattling the air as the sun tucks itself away behind the treetops.

In the darkness, J.D.'s vision is slightly affected, the only time his missing eye becomes a problem; but it's far from pitch black out. There's still a hint of light peeping through the leaves, enough for things to still appear somewhat three-dimensional.

"Tell us where it is!" Abram yells, his gun in one of the Goons' faces.

"Where what is?" Goon #1 replies, a thin guy with greasy blond hair.

"Do you take me for a fuckin' sap?" Abram yells, the master of ceremonies for this show. He's entered into some gangster movie now, preening and elucidating each syllable for prime impact.

"Body bags or kneecapping, fellas?" Abram asks. "Those are your two options."

"Wedon'tknowwhatyerafter," Goon #1 cries.

"All right, let's start with kneecapping and see if that changes your mind."

Abram fires a bullet in Goon #1's left knee. The guy lets out a scream that never seems to stop. J.D. knows that getting shot in the knee is one of the most painful places imaginable due to all the bone, cartilage, muscle fibers and nerve bundles in a small area.

"Next time I aim for an organ. Now we know you're hiding a fuck ton of blow so make this easy on yourself."

Goon #2 has broken down in tears. He's younger than Goon #1, maybe still in his teens.

"The bricks are sown into the seat cushions," the guy murmurs.

"Craig!" Goon #1 yells, ropes of spit dribbling down his neck.

Abram nods at Twin #1 to check.

Twin #1 takes out a pocketknife and slices the seat cushions. Bricks and bricks of white candy a plenty. He starts removing them from the cushions.

Goon #1 is losing a lot of blood. He's got his hands over the wound, but it isn't helping much. It looks like all the blood has drained from his face that's white as snow now.

"I'm bleeding out over here," he says, writhing in pain, imploring for Abram to have mercy.

Abram's circling around Goon #1, loving every minute of this.

"I always say an injured dog needs to be put down."

He stops in his tracks and fires a bullet into Goon #1's skull.

The guy slumps over as Goon #2 starts begging for God to save him.

J.D. isn't shocked, knowing Abram wasn't ever planning on letting these guys live. Easier to kill a threat than to worry about looking over your shoulder. He's aware that Abram might have the same plan for him, or even have Peanut do the deed, especially once the copious amount of bricks are removed from the van.

Goon #2 has gone into full church parishioner

mode, flip-flopping around on the dirt, pleading with the heavens for his safety.

Abram steps over him, the gun between the guy's eyes.

"Please, please. I didn't see nothing here–"

Abram squeezes the trigger and another body slumps to the ground.

"Put them both in the van," Abram orders the Twins. "No one will find them all the way out here for days."

The Twins each drag one of the Goons and dump them into the van, two streaks of blood left as a trail.

"Very good, fellas, very good," Abram says, nodding at his success.

Twin #1 starts picking up the bricks of coke and stuffing them into his coat.

"Woo hoo," Peanut whistles, his eyes bigger than ever. "That was w-w-wild."

Peanut's skinny body does a jig, dipping and weaving around the coke like a hippie at a bonfire.

"Told ya I know how to set shit up," Abram says, and howls at the rising moon.

J.D. watches their celebration. It's all been too easy. But The Doctor is the biggest wildcard. He won't allow himself to celebrate like them until he's in a plane overlooking the ocean.

Twin #1 puts the last brick of coke in his coat.

"Man," Peanut says, slapping his forehead. "Look at the amount those goons had on them. We're looking at some kind of bank–"

A gunshot goes off. For a second, J.D. thinks it's from someone who followed them, but then he watches Peanut keel over.

Twin #2 stands there with a smoking gun and an *I couldn't help it* expression before turning the gun on Abram.

Twin #1 draws on J.D., who points his gun right back.

"What in the living hell is going on?" Abram shouts.

"You, Abram, are about as trustworthy as a raccoon around a pile of garbage," Twin #2 says.

"You were aiming to do the same thing to us," Twin #1 agrees. "That's why you brought the eye patch in on this."

"Boys, you have me all wrong. I was gonna split the cash five ways, swear to it."

They all look at Peanut.

"Okay, I'm set on splitting it *four* ways now," Abram says. "We still can."

The Twins glance at each other, shake their heads.

"Or we can just take the blow to The Doctor on our own and divide it in two," Twin #2 says.

"But I'm the connection!"

"Think The Doctor gives a shit about you?" Twin #1 laughs. "You're just a fly he's been waiting to swat."

"So both of you just go ahead and drop your guns now," says Twin #2.

"You're just gonna shoot us anyway, you fat fucks," Abram yells.

"Yeah, you right."

Twin #2 fires, the bullet catching Abram in the hand that's holding the gun, bones shattering and getting pulled right out of the hand, the bullet passing right through.

Abram screams like a child, his wail echoing

through the woods. He wraps his sleeve around his mutilated hand.

"You goddamn cocksuckers." He turns to J.D. "Marcus, don't put down that gun."

J.D. keeps alternating his aim between the two Twins. He didn't see this coming, focusing too much on the notion that Abram would be the one to turn, or even Peanut. The Twins weren't even on his radar. Maybe reuniting with Annie made him sloppy, a sliver of his brain locked on her where it should've all been directed towards his goal.

This is not how he expected his endgame to turn out. Dead in the woods by the hand of someone other than the Desire Card.

"Drop that motherfucking gun," both Twins shout.

J.D. assesses the situation. In his mind, a Debussy concerto is playing, something to keep him as calm as possible so he can assess the situation. *Deux Arabesques*, a melodic façade to drown out the grim scene. If he fires at one Twin, the other is sure to clip him. There's a slim chance he could fire two shots in time, but the Twins are standing pretty far apart. He has no other choice but to lower the gun.

"Goddamnit, Marcus, what are you doing?" Abram wails.

J.D. catches Abram's eye. *Shut the fuck up, moron. This is my rodeo.*

Each Twin bends down to pick up a gun from the ground.

In the nanosecond they take their eye off J.D., he swipes the Kamikaze Knife from his waistband and lunges at Twin #2. Slashes the guy's throat, blood spurting out like a busted fire hydrant. Then he goes for

Twin #1 who fumbles his gun. A shot goes off, but it only hits a tree.

J.D. raises the knife and plunges it into Twin #1's chest. One of the bricks that Twin #1 stuffed in his coat explodes. White powder everywhere.

Twin #1 grabs J.D.'s arm, sinks his teeth in like a dog, a bloody mouth print as a gift.

J.D. growls in pain and yanks the knife out of Twin #1's chest.

Twin #1 holds his hands up in defense. "No, no!"

J.D. stabs the blade into the guy's right eye, works it in good. He pulls the blade out, leaving Twin #1 thrashing around in a bloody puddle. Soon Twin #1 stops moving.

"C'mon, let's grab everything and get the hell out of here."

Abram is too stunned to move.

"Fuck, Abram, let's go."

He yanks open Twin #1's coat and begins tossing the bricks of coke into a pile.

Abram slinks down and picks up a brick, sticks his nose in and takes a good whiff.

"Hoo boy," Abram says, slapping his cheeks with his maimed hand, still in a daze. "Glad you're on my side, Marcus."

Abram's scruffy face is a vision of blood and white powder all mixed together, a perfect summation of what they all just went through.

And the day is far from over yet.

31

"THAT FAT FUCKER SHOT OFF MY FINGERS, MY goddamn fingers!" Abram howls in the pick-up over to The Doctor's. Seems like he's snapped out of his daze and is in complete freak-out mode now. He holds up his mutilated hand, three of the five fingers hanging on for dear life, the other two blown off somewhere in the woods.

J.D. blinks and finds himself back in Marrakesh. He's in his hotel room, opening up the box left for him at the front desk. Inside he finds ten chopped off fingers swirling in a pool of blood. Everything goes out of focus: the fingers, the room.

He blinks again and is back in the car, swerving out of the way to avoid a fallen tree branch.

He thinks of all the death that has followed him throughout his life starting with his parents on that icy road, to the woman and her baby in Siniyah, to the countless marks he's had to extinguish until he finally refused to assassinate one. Not like it mattered anyway. Hasan Bouchtat suffered an even worse death at the hands of another operative. Had J.D. gone through with the kill, the guy would've just gotten a quick bullet to his brain.

"Those motherfuckin' hippos," Abram cries, bashing his hand against the ceiling, blood splattering everywhere.

"Keep that hand wrapped up in your sleeve."

Abram's eyes are rising into his skull. Uh-oh, too much blood leaking out. Even though J.D. could give a shit whether Abram lives or dies, he doesn't want to head into The Doctor's place solo.

"I knew you came along for a reason," Abram says, his voice getting softer with each word. "Showing up in town, bedding my—"

Abram slumps over in his seat, his head smacking against the dash.

"Ah, shit," J.D. mutters, and reaches back to pinch some coke from one of the bricks. He jams a heavily powdered finger up Abram's nose.

Abram jolts up, as if a puppeteer is controlling his movements from up above.

"But those tubs of lard have been plotting against me this whole time. Undermining my authority, only out for themselves. Goddamn pieces of pig shit."

J.D. pins him back against the seat.

"You can't trust no one but yourself," Abram continues, snot dripping from his nose. "Everyone is out to get you eventually. The question is when, Marcus? When will they catch up and gut you?"

"Shut up."

"Gutted and thrown back in the ocean. Left to rot till the maggots ravish you. That one eye you got left hollowed out."

J.D. jerks the wheel in a fit of anger, causing Abram to knock his head against the window.

"Get it together," J.D. says, gritting his teeth until he can taste bone shards. "We still have The Doctor to deal with, understand? This isn't fucking over yet."

A flicker of reason behind Abram's eyes. He lowers his chin and nods, blows a red snot rocket into his good hand.

J.D. guns the gas as the pick-up barrels down the road, the image of those mutilated fingers still swirling in his head.

## 32

J.D. AND A VISIBLY BLOODY ABRAM ENTER THE circus of The Doctor's house with the bricks of coke in a garbage bag. Naked underlings swish around: cutting up coke and weighing it, feeding bills through a counting machine. No one seems to notice them except for the two linebacker guards at the door who insist on taking their guns. They pat J.D. down but somehow miss the Kamikaze Knife in his waistband.

The Doctor sits on his throne, his hair pulled back into a ponytail and greased to stay in place. Purple sunglasses hiding his eyes. He's wearing a beach shirt full of palm trees that's open at the neck to reveal a tuft of gray coils, the skin underneath fried to a crisp. He uses the long fingernail on his pinky to scoop some coke from a silver platter at his side. After a sniff, he notices Abram and J.D.

"What the fuck is this?" The Doctor growls. "You're dripping blood all over my shag."

Abram looks down at the small puddle that has formed on The Doctor's carpet.

"Yeah, we kinda hit a snag."

"You got the goods?

J.D. holds up the garbage bag.

"Then I'll take No Fingers over here in the back to clean him up."

The Doctor rises from his throne and leads Abram into a room.

J.D. sits on a couch between two naked underlings who are busy sorting heaps of drugs into little baggies. There's a diligence to their work, as if they're being monitored at all times, as if a second of rest could be fatal. He recognizes one of them, the young man with the slick hair that The Doctor smacked around before, the bruise on his cheek noticeable.

"I could help you," he says, indicating the baggies.

The guy doesn't look up.

"No, you can't," the guy finally says, taking his offer the wrong way, refusing to believe that a hero can exist. He licks the inside of his bruise, seems sad enough to dissolve.

J.D. wants to tell him that they share a history: a chained similarity, a Boss who refuses to let them go, a life of servitude and sin. He wants to tell him to run, to never look back and hide in the crevices until he's far enough away. But that probably wouldn't save him anyway. For the world isn't very big and monsters like Gable and The Doctor are persistent. They've built successful empires because they refuse to fail. So that is why this guy sits nude on a couch cutting up drugs with a bruise down his cheek rather than forging a real life he could be proud of, one where he is free.

The guy has made a choice, as has J.D. And who's to say which is the smarter option? A bullet to the head may be his inevitable future. A future that could even be moments away.

———

After some time, Abram emerges from a back room with his hand sewn and bandaged. He's been given some kind of sedative, but it looks like it's just balanced out all the other stuff in his system.

The Doctor steps out of the room as well and takes off a pair of bloody latex gloves. Tosses them in the trash.

"Good thing I once had a medical license," he says, returning to his throne. "You lost two digits but you'll live."

A naked girl waits on The Doctor with a silver tray of coke. He complies with a sniff. Claps his hands and moves his body to a beat in his head. Glances around perplexed.

"What happened to your two massive associates, Frick and Frack?"

Abram indicates the bandaged hand. "Guess they had their own plan."

"They're insignificant now," J.D. says, the first thing he's said to The Doctor since they arrived.

"Well then, let's see what you brought me, Patch."

J.D. opens the garbage bag full of the bricks.

The Doctor peers inside, no indication if he's pleased or not. He waves over one of his naked underlings.

"Laurita, *ven aqui*."

Laurita slinks over, a coy smile on her face, heavy blue shadow and white lipstick like some 6os pin-up.

The Doctor takes out a pocketknife and stabs one of the bricks. He holds out the blade for Laurita with a bump's worth.

Laurita bends down with one finger blocking a nostril.

"No baby, you know how I like to test it."

The Doctor wets his index finger and dips it into the coke.

Laurita opens her mouth and sucks the Doctor's coke finger. She tingles as she releases it from her lips.

"*Ay Papi*, it's good, it's good."

The Doctor rubs the coke residue across his bloody gums. The music in his head accelerating, his body jerking around like he's having a mini-seizure. Finally, he sits still, turns to Abram and J.D.

"Looks like your candy cane passed the test."

He picks up a remote and turns on some music. "Take On Me" by A-Ha. The Doctor likes what he likes. He sings along, off-key and mangling the words while weighing each brick of coke.

J.D. glances around nervously, his hand millimeters away from the Kamikaze Knife just in case. The two guards are at the door packing Smith & Wesson M&P22s, a serviceable gun but it's uncertain how good a shot they are. Tucked in the groove of The Doctor's throne, J.D. also notices an old school pistol.

Abram is chewing the hell out of his lip, tapping his foot like a junkie. He looks over at J.D., but J.D.'s keeping his good eye on The Doctor, tracking the guy's slightest movements should he reach for the pistol.

"So you knuckleheads actually came through," The Doctor says, as he finishes weighing the last brick. "Here's your take."

He tosses J.D. a gym bag. J.D. unzips it to find stacks and stacks of cash. More than enough to get him to Fiji and beyond.

The Doctor raises the volume on the stereo, sings along.

> *"You're shying away...*
> *I'll be coming for you anyway.*
> *Take on me, take me on.*
> *You'll be gone, in a day or two-o-o-..."*

In a flash, The Doctor lunges for the pistol. Cocks it and gives a shit-eating grin. Points it at Abram and J.D., switching off between the two.

"Oh hell," Abram says.

J.D. slowly reaches in his waistband for the knife, minimal motions, nothing too suspect. He can feel the cold handle finally. He'll be ready if need be.

The Doctor lowers the pistol with a cackle. "Couldn't resist. Did you all see their faces?"

The naked underlings all cackle too, their forced laughs clogging the room.

"This one nearly shit himself," The Doctor says, pointing at Abram.

"Fuck yeah, I think I really did," Abram says. "Kind of day I've had."

"But you were ready," The Doctor says to J.D. "I could see it in that one eye of yours. You've got a knife down your pants with my name on it. You're ready for whatever's thrown at you, aren't you, Patch?"

J.D.'s still a little shaken, but he'd never show his shot nerves. Over the years he's gotten good at tempering them, never allowing the tiniest bit of sweat to be visible.

He stares The Doctor down, this man who represents everything he's running from. He longs to whip out the knife and go gutting, but instead he nods, and by doing so, saves them all.

"Now get the fuck out of my house, you scum-sucking douche rags."

J.D. and Abram back out as "Take On Me" starts up again and The Doctor continues his serenade.

# 33

J.D.'s DRIVING THE PICK-UP AWAY FROM THE
Doctor's place, screwing the speed limit by flooring the
gas. Abram's in shotgun, moaning about some kind of
nonsense. The guy snorts another bump of candy,
regurgitating his monologue about being scared shitless.
But J.D. knew The Doctor wasn't going to ice them,
especially after taking the time to bandage Abram's
wound. Sociopaths like The Doctor just refuse to make
things easy. J.D. almost wanted The Doctor to try something. He's been running on adrenaline since the inci-
dent with the Twins and the Goons. It was a shame it
had to go to waste.

Abram's holding onto his gun in his good hand. He's
waving it around like a fool and it's starting to make J.D.
nervous.

"So how do I get to Annie's from here?" J.D. asks,
making sure that Abram focuses on the rest of The
Plan.

"She's on Old Stanton Drive, Marcus. But you
know how to get there, don't you?"

"...What's that supposed to mean?" J.D. has his good eye on the road, unable to see Abram's reaction. "Are you trying to imply something, Abram?"

"Oh, I ain't implying. You've spent quite some time at Annie's place if I'm correct."

The gun barrel moves into J.D.'s periphery. Fuck, shit, goddamn. Another scum-sucker shows his true colors.

"You fucked her, didn't you, Marcus? Fucked her on those same sheets that she and I shared, fucked her all over the house so everywhere I look all I'll see is pieces of you."

J.D. continues concentrating on the road. The knife is in his waistband, the gun in a pocket. Neither is an option driving at this speed.

"Is that why you're gonna kill me and keep all the cash, Abram? You'll tell yourself it's ok because I got with your girl? I saved your life, man. You'd be plugged with holes in the woods if not for me."

"Oh Marcus, you've got things all twisted, my brother. Annie fucked you 'cause I told her to. Since she's always been good at getting some sap to do her dirty work. And that's all you are...a sap. A dead sap."

J.D. yanks the steering wheel to his right, causing Abram to be thrown back. He lets go of the wheel to grapple for the gun.

The pick-up swerves from lane to lane. A car coming from the other direction almost hits them.

Abram fires the gun, shooting a bullet through the roof.

J.D. grabs hold of the wheel with one hand and punches Abram in the face. Crunch of bone and cartilage as he does it again and again. Abram's nose becomes all bloody and looks jammed in the wrong direction.

"What about Annie's bruises?" J.D. asks. "Was it just make-up, or did you hit her like that so I'd feel bad and do anything she said?"

"What do you think, shithead?"

J.D. pops Abram one last time in the face, then he goes for the gun that's fallen onto the seat. He spins it around so it's pointing at Abram's stomach.

Abram lunges for the barrel, tries with all his might to move it away.

"Tell me the truth," J.D. yells, fighting to keep the gun steady. "Was she really playing me?"

"Don't shoot me, Marcus. We're a team you and I. The cash can be split between both of us, brother. More than you expected to get. In fact, I'll make it 60/40 in your favor. You can step outta this truck with the bulk of it and never have to see me again."

A few stitches on Abram's hand begin to open up. He squeals and lets go of the gun.

"Okay, okay," he cries, curling up in a ball and waving his bandaged hand in front of his face. "70/30 and you keep the pick-up. Toss me out with a few bills and no hard feelings."

J.D. disengages the safety.

"Goddamnit, Marcus, you kill me and you'll never know if I was telling the truth about Annie!"

J.D. plugs Abram in the belly. Abram lets out a whimper as his guts ooze out.

J.D. looks around for other cars coming by. He opens up the side door and kicks Abram out. He watches in the rearview as Abram flies out of the truck and rolls off the road down a steep hill. He closes the side door and puts both hands on the wheel, catching his breath. He can't help but remember when he and Annie were lying in bed together the other night. He had asked her to come with him to Matagi Island and she got really quiet.

"We both know that ain't likely," she finally said.

"What's keeping you here?"

"I've given up, J.D. I'm not good no more. I haven't been in a while. A place like Killenroy is all that'll have me."

We do what we must when we run out of options. When life has become nothing more than turmoil, and we can only see one way out. Annie may have seen an opportunity the moment J.D. knocked on her door after eight years without a word. Her one chance to escape Killenroy and the dregs she associated with. But if she was playing him she had to have been playing Abram as well. That girl was wily enough to want the prize all for herself. Everyone else in her way would be knocked down and forgotten.

She was more like J.D. than she knew.

But there could be a chance that Abram was lying. That he found out she'd been fucking around on him and wanted to save face. Once J.D. gets to Old Stanton Drive, he'll have to stick a gun in Annie's temple to see if fear of death could bring out the truth.

Could he ever trust her again, even if he believes her story? Or would a shred of him always wonder, always be looking over his shoulder to check if she's sharpening her nails, ready to strike?

He'll just have to wait and see her reaction first before he decides how to proceed.

# 34

SMELLING OF CORDITE, A BLOODY J.D. PULLS UP TO Annie's place. He's running on impulse and rage, unable to make a sound judgment. He flings a piece of Abram's gut off his finger as he parks the pick-up. Another body to add to the pile of those whose lives he took: some sinners in their own right, others simply unlucky. Which deaths would he have to account for when his own life ends? Who deserved their fate and who will haunt him in eternity? Abram's was certainly warranted, but what about Annie? How grave are her sins?

With the gun in one hand and the gym bag in the other, he heads to her door. Knocks hard.

He can hear the shuffling of feet inside. She takes a moment too long to answer. Did she see him through the window? Is she stalling?

When she opens the door, her face reveals genuine shock. She takes in the fresh blood, the random bits of flesh hanging from his clothes. She puts a quivering hand over her mouth.

"J.D., what happened?"

He barrels inside, slams the door shut. "They're all dead. The Twins shot Peanut and then I took them out."

"What about Abram?" she asks, peering out the window.

J.D. tries to read her. Clear panic is reflected in her eyes, but what else?

"Your boyfriend tried to kill me. I left him on the side of the road with a bullet in his stomach."

"Abram's dead?"

"But you knew he was gonna turn on me, didn't you?"

"W-what do you mean?"

He drops the gym bag to grab her by the shoulders.

"Abram told me the plan you two had. That I was just some sap you've been conning all along."

"No, J.D., I swear–"

There's a boiling anger inside of him. He shakes her hard enough to give her whiplash.

"You think you can tease me like that? Make me have real feelings about someone for once? You money grubbing..."

He raises his hand to smack her.

"What're you gonna do? You gonna hit me just like Abram used to?"

She's crying now, crocodile tears most likely.

"Just tell me the truth, Annie. All of it!"

"I wasn't gonna con you. I only told Abram what he wanted to hear because he refused to listen." She licks her lips very slowly. "He was aiming to take all the cash, but I was gonna talk him out of it."

"That's a load of bullshit."

"But what happened between us these last few days wasn't bullshit. Fiji? Running away to paradise? I can't tell you how much I wanted that."

She nuzzles her cheek against his fingers like a cat would. Her tears are still coming, gobs and gobs of them.

"Abram never told me nothin' about tryin' to kill you. Maybe just scare you a bit so you'd let him have all the cash, but not kill you."

"It might have helped to let me know that, Annie."

"And I was gonna give you some of my cut anyway, no matter what happened. Really, I was. Or I was even thinkin' of takin' it all from Abram and heading to the airport with you. I hadn't decided yet. Well, I mean I did decide I wanted to go with you, I just wasn't sure about takin' everything from Abram."

"You said you'd never leave Killenroy."

"That was before I thought we really had a shot of gettin' outta here. But then I began to dream about it. You and me on a never-ending beach. The past few days I've been wakin' up with the taste of salt on my tongue." She glances downward, a sadness overwhelming her. "But none of that matters now."

"What do you mean, 'none of that matters now'?"

J.D. hears a sound coming from the hallway. A quiet footstep.

"Who's in the hallway, Annie?"

"I'm so sorry, J.D. I didn't have no choice."

Carmen emerges from the shadows of the hallway with a rifle in hand. Red hair pulled back into a pony-tail. Her nipped and tucked face even more inhuman than usual.

"Drop the gun and kick over the bag now," she says, cocking the rifle.

# 35

EVEN THOUGH IT'S HARD TO SEE ANY EMOTION ON Carmen's plastic face, J.D. can tell she's not fucking around. The rifle is a few feet away from his skull, one shot and his head explodes. She's too far out of reach to swipe with the knife in his waistband so he lowers the gun and kicks over the gym bag.

Keeping her eye on both of them, Carmen bends down like a baseball catcher and unzips the bag. She smiles once she sees the cash, the first real emotion she's shown.

"Very nice." She zips up the bag and rises to her feet.

"What's going on here?" J.D. asks.

"I'm surprised you don't remember me," Carmen says. "Maybe it would help if you pictured burns all over my face?"

He blinks and sees the support group in Newburgh after he returned from Iraq. All of them sitting in a circle. The Woman with a Burned Face taps him on the shoulder.

"Recognize me now?" Burned Face asks, and he's zapped back to reality.

"*Rita.*"

"Weren't you the one who told me to get skin grafts, Dean?" she says. "Well, Gable promised me them if I went after you. Gave me some new procedure that had results in minutes. And look how I fooled you. You didn't have a clue who I was."

She's right. He had let his mind drift in Killenroy, but the Card had always been there: watching, plotting.

"Why didn't you kill me already, Rita? You had the chance. Could've got me right outside the bar after I left. I wouldn't have seen it coming. Weren't we told by the great fucking Gable to always knife them in the back? To never let them see it coming?"

"I know I could've iced you outside the bar, Dean."

"That's not my name."

"Oh right, you go rogue and the name just disappears? All of a sudden, you're Storm again? That's not how it works. What you are is dead. And your grave will say Dean."

"So why am I still alive? You've got a perfect success rate, no mark left standing–"

"*We* had a perfect success rate. You and I and the station agent James Cagney, Gable's #2. No one else at the main office. Not Bogart, not Jimmy Stewart, not even that up-and-comer Mae West."

"Only you and Cagney have that perfect success rate now."

"I never thought you'd be a mark, Dean."

Her face still shows no emotion, a mannequin with a gun.

"I thought one day we'd be retired on some island Gable bought for all of us," she says.

"It would never all end that way."

She sucks her teeth in and spits out the words, "I guess you'll never find out."

"So you don't need the Rita Hayworth mask anymore now that you've got a new face?"

He intends to keep asking questions, anything to stall time.

"I'll keep her hidden for this kill."

"So do it already. Fucking end me. What are you trying to prove?"

"I'm not trying to prove anything. I kept you alive because Blondie over here told me about your drug heist. Figured I'd make some extra cash."

"I just thought I made a new friend," Annie mumbles.

"You can let us go, Rita. Take all of the cash and tell Gable you couldn't find me. Give me a head start."

"He'd never believe that. Jimmy Stewart saw you get into that truck back in Vermont. We had you tracked. More operatives are headed this way as we speak."

The rage inside of him builds up again, boils over, spilling out of his ears.

"One day Gable's gonna make you do something so vile, so corrupt, so demonic that you won't be able to go through with it. Then you'll be in the same position as me. This will happen to all the operatives at some point. Everyone has a line they won't cross. They have to."

"Only the weak ones do. And that's why you're being hunted. It's why we can't let you live. I'm loyal, Dean. The Card is my family. And I would die for it.

Because of Gable I'm not a fucking mutant anymore. So I'd travel all the way to Hell for him. I know I'm headed there eventually."

"He made us into murderers."

"You were one already, soldier."

A growl erupts from Annie as she charges at Rita.

The gun goes off as the two women spiral to the floor, the bullet shattering a window.

Rita and Annie grapple for the rifle. Finally, Rita gets a hold of it.

A shot rings out clipping Rita in the arm. J.D. has his smoking gun pointed at her head.

"Tell me everything you know about Gable."

Rita clamps a hand over the bullet wound. Brings her breathing down from a panic to a cool hum.

"I know he will keep coming after you."

"That is why he's my next target. That's why none of the other operatives matter. I ice the Boss and the fucking game ends. So how can I find him?"

"Why should I tell you anything if you'll just kill me anyway?"

"Because you get to choose how you'll die, Rita. I can make it quick and painless. Or I can do to you what was done to me."

He flips up the eye patch to show his mutilated socket.

"All right, all right," she says, seething. A hiss coming from her lips. "I don't know the Boss's real name or anything, you won't get that from me. Or what he looks like. No one knows. He's always worn the Gable mask."

"Where is he now?"

"What will you do to my face?"

"I'm not fucking around, Rita. Where is that psychotic son-of-a-bitch?"

"Kill me, kill me because I won't tell. He'll know I did. He'll hunt me down even after I'm dead. He'll find me in whatever Hell exists afterwards."

J.D. picks her up by the neck as she wiggles around. He lets go to take the Kamikaze Knife out of his waistband.

"I will peel that travesty you call a face right off. Do you understand? You will wish you only had burns after I'm done."

Now Rita trembles, her whole body convulsing.

He puts the knife up to her cheek so she can see her reflection. The blade cutting into skin.

"All right, all right!"

He steps away as she succumbs to a coughing fit.

"I'll tell you everything I know," she says, wiping spittle from her lips. "Just don't touch my face. Promise me you'll leave my face alone. Promise me!"

He nods.

"Gable's...in Macau right now. He's dealing with some casino he's building. Says it will be the tallest in the world."

"What's the name?"

"I wasn't briefed with the name."

"What hotel is he staying at?"

"Only the operatives traveling with him know that information."

"How will I find him?"

"His son is there as well."

"He has a son?"

"I overheard a conversation Gable had the other day on his headset. I was supposed to be monitoring

Astaire because he's been off since his surgery, but I bugged the wrong room. It was one of those empty rooms, you know the ones that Gable insist stay empty? It was late at night and I wandered into it by accident. You know how he requests the lights to be off after a certain hour. Anyway, when I listened to the tape later he had been in there on his headset. It sounded like a family matter."

"He has a family?"

"I think we've all suspected so. That he goes home and takes off his mask and is a pillar of the community. A successful businessman with a wife, kids, maybe even grandkids, dogs on the front lawn, a perfect cover."

"Is this son who's in Macau an operative? If Gable has a family, they couldn't know what he does."

"He's not an operative. He's in trouble. That's why Gable brought him all the way to Macau. He plans on leaving him there. Apparently, the son spends his time getting fucked up on crystal at gay clubs. A few weeks ago, he messed up a one-night stand pretty bad and the twink is in a coma. Parents are pressing charges. Gable doesn't want him dead, but he wants to erase him, as in the son won't exist anymore. Gable was on the headset with the international office. The Boss there must be helping him out."

"So find the son and have him lead me to Gable? What else did he say about him? A name? Any physical descriptions?"

"No name but the son has white hair."

"Like an albino?"

"I don't know, just that his hair is white. That was how Gable described him. A chubby man in his forties with hair as white as bleach."

"How the fuck will I even begin to find him?"

"Macau isn't too gay friendly, but I imagine his son still likes to party despite what he's going through. There can't be too many gay clubs to choose from."

"What if Gable's not even letting him outside?"

"Gable is too busy with the casino deal right now. That's what he was stressing on the headset. That was what the call was all about. The son was almost an aside. He just wants him set up there and out of his hair."

"Anything else?"

She thinks for a moment, a long stretched out lull. Maybe she wants that minute because she knows she won't have many more. She shakes her head.

"I can't let you live," he sighs. "I need a leg-up on the Card. I can't have them know you told me what you did."

Rita's eyes start to water. "I can't have that either."

He raises the gun.

"Will you shoot me in the chest? I don't want the blood to touch my face."

"Was that new face worth dying for in the end?"

She nods. Takes a deep breath to prepare.

He sticks the gun between her eyes and fires. She slumps to the floor, a surprise gasp on her face.

Annie runs over to him, hysterical. "Oh, J.D!"

He's still staring at Rita's corpse.

"She was so sweet when I met her," Annie cries. "She really cared to listen about Abram and talk with me about how she'd been abused too."

"It's because she was abused. We were all fucking abused. I was abused."

"Are you gonna go to this Macau place?"

"I have to if I want to stay alive."

"Well...what about the money? I know you can't fly with that much cash. TSA is gonna ask you about it and figure out that something criminal has been going on."

"Keep it. Just leave me enough for plane tickets and a little extra."

He steps toward the gym bag, but she grabs his arm.

"No, J.D., I don't want it. I mean, I wanna share it with you. I still want to be with you."

It's hard to gauge whether she being honest or not, but he realizes he has nothing to lose. She's right that he can't fly with that kind of cash. He might as well take her at her word. Even now after sticking a gun in her face and wishing her the worst, he feels a magnetic charge between them, along with a heavenly whiff of lemon, all reasons to believe that the two of them could be rolling around on a beach together if the future gives them a break.

"I can hold onto the rest of the money while you go to Macau, J.D. Put it in a bank account and meet you on that island you talked about."

"How do I know you'll really meet me?"

"You just have to trust me."

She steps over Rita's body, wraps her arms around him.

"I'm the same girl you always thought I was. Just lookin' for any chance I have to get away from this place. Please be my chance, J.D."

"It's Marcus Edmonton," he says. "J.D. Storm's been dead for some time. He has to be."

"All right...Marcus."

She gives him a twisted grin. Starts kissing his neck.

He's cold at first, but then begins rubbing her back with his free hand.

"You and me in paradise," Annie whispers.

He kisses her passionately. They look demented with blood splattered all over them and a dead girl on the floor, but all he's concentrating on is that kiss and whether he believes it to be real. If he can feel it all the way to his toes.

He pulls away, a little knock-kneed, and goes over to the gym bag. Takes out a few stacks of bills and stuffs them in his pockets.

"Matagi Island," he says. "Give me about a week to take care of what I need to do. Walk up and down the beach every day when you get there. If I make it out of Macau alive, I'll find you."

"Okay."

She runs over and kisses him again. Punctures his lip from kissing him too hard.

"Sorry."

"I hope you surprise me, Annie. I really do."

He licks away the blood and slowly backs up out of the door, taking in this last vision of Annie, all wide-eyed and splattered with red.

## PART THREE

# FOR THEY WERE
# SAVAGES, ALL OF THEM

# 36

The closest town with a train station that'll take Marcus Edmonton to the Seattle-Tacoma International Airport is Bellingham, a two and a half hour ride. He'd rather take a bus than a cab to Bellingham, since his life may depend on being surrounded by as many people as possible. Killenroy doesn't have a bus depot but Junction does, so he slings his pack over his shoulder and hoofs it there.

Annie's on his mind during the walk over, even though he tries to focus and forget about her for now. She creeps into his thoughts, makes room for herself in his cranium, sets up shop and refuses to budge. Is this love? All he can say is that it's torture, for the likelihood of the two of them winding up together is slim.

Junction's bus depot is a crime scene waiting to happen. The tang of urine in the air. The building looking like a heavy wind might blow it to pieces. The nighttime bringing out the worst of the junkies, men and women who've made the place their home, the floors littered with needles.

He steps over an entwined couple so he can buy a ticket from the machine. They're shivering from the cold, each with blue lips, eyes that can no longer cry. The woman is too high to acknowledge the towering stranger stepping over her, but the man grabs Marcus's foot. Marcus gives a swift kick to the guy's head, a knee-jerk reaction. The guy mewls and curls up with his woman, both of them lost beyond repair. The woman has a Mariners baseball cap that Marcus swipes, the smell putrid but he will put it on and place it low over his eyes. He buys the ticket and heads outside to wait for the bus.

There's another man waiting, the only other non-junkie at the depot. The man has a crooked nose and gives Marcus a quick glance before looking away. Marcus had cleaned up at a gas station along the way but a swipe of blood still runs down his arm. His best solution is to flip his coat inside out so he does so.

It's too foggy out to see a moon so he must adjust his good eye to the dark. He's got the crooked nose man in his sights just in case the guy is an operative, but he's also making sure to scan the area for any surprises. If the Card knew Rita was dead, he'd be dead too, which means they haven't found out yet. Which buys him a drop of time.

After ten or so minutes, the bus appears in the distance, two giant beams of yellow light flooding the road. It parks as Marcus and Crooked Nose get on. He walks down the aisle, observing each rider. Nine in total. Crooked Nose crumples into the first row of seats and leans against the window, nodding off. Behind him is a granny with a sour face. Behind her a teenage girl in shorts. To the right a stocky man in a straw porkpie hat, also sleeping. In the back of the bus sits a large black woman with an old black man and a suburban-looking mom to their left. So far none seem like operatives, although he knows it's foolish to generalize. For this mission, Gable may have hired the most unassuming trainees yet.

The bus takes off, turning onto the highway. The trip is less than an hour, but will feel like a lifetime. If the Card has found out about Rita's death by then, there's bound to be an operative at the Bellingham train station, since it's the fastest way to get to Seattle. They may not know that he's planning on going to Macau, but they will figure he's headed somewhere by plane.

He wants to shut his eyes for a quick nap, but he can't. To sleep is to die, that will be his new rule until he reaches Macau.

## 37

Once the bus stops in Bellingham, it's a mile walk to the train station. Marcus checks the arrivals and sees that he has two hours, better to walk over than have to wait at a station for too long. Beautiful town, leagues from the dregs he just came from: snow-capped mini mountains banking the area, the greenest trees he's seen since Vermont. The air fresh, rejuvenating, life-altering, a smell of pine as a finish.

At the train station, a few of the bus riders take up the benches. The large black woman with the old man. The girl in shorts, odd for this time of year. Granny too. No sign of Crooked Nose, Suburban Mom, or the guy in the porkpie hat. He buys his ticket and a bag of peanuts from the vending machine. Munches while standing.

It's hot in the station, the heater turned to the max, so he makes his way outside for another hit of fresh air. No one else waits outside, the cold too much of a deterrent.

As he eats more peanuts, he hears the crunch of

gravel behind him. The girl in shorts has stepped outside chewing on a piece of bubble gum. She blows a giant pink bubble that's begging to pop but it keeps getting bigger and bigger. Finally, it bursts and he feels a gun pressed into the small of his back. A gloved hand covers his mouth. The shorts girl trots away as he spins around to see his executioner.

The man in the straw porkpie hat.

A gust of wind sweeps the hat off of the guy's head and Marcus recognizes Omar Sharif, one of the international operatives. A neat mustache with serious eyes and a cleft chin.

"Hands in the air and start walking," Omar Sharif says, pushing him with the gun.

"Where are we walking?"

"Away from the station, behind that batch of trees."

They make their way through the line of trees in the back of the station until they cannot be seen. Omar confiscates Marcus's gun, finds the trusty Kamikaze Knife as well. No weapons to speak of anymore.

"We haven't heard from Hayworth in too long," Omar's robotic voice says. There's a hint of excitement to his tone, the thrill of being the operative to finally bring James Dean down. "We must assume she is dead."

"She is."

Omar rubs his mustache, a nervous tic, maybe even a hint of remorse. Rita probably seduced him as well at some point. She must've gone through them all.

"Does Gable want me dead or alive?" Marcus asks, stalling for time again, his mind ablaze with any possible way to save himself.

"Deader than dead. I was on an assignment from

Olivier at the international office when your case took precedence. Gable had a feeling that you've wanted to run for some time. You eluded me in Marrakesh, but you will not elude me here."

"You were in the Es Saadi Palace hotel," Marcus says. "The Middle Eastern man watching me in the lobby."

Omar taps his nose and nods.

"Egyptian to be precise," he says. "Just like Omar Sharif. I was fated to become him. Just as I am fated to end you."

Marcus flicks a stray peanut around his mouth. "And what will happen when you do?"

"Likely a transfer, bumped up from operative to station agent."

"Congratulations."

"We never worked together before, Dean–"

"That's not my name!"

"But we share a kinship. A similar defect. Although mine was at birth, an eye entirely made of iris without a pupil."

"Let me see."

"And lose my focus for a second and give you a chance to overpower me? I know your record too well. Gable had proficiently trained you in Savate, Muy Thai, and Brazilian Ju-Jitsu, as well as your sniper abilities. At this moment, you are thinking about twelve different ways to kill me, but I am a step ahead of you because I know all of them as well."

"Then why isn't there a bullet between my eyes already?"

"Because I want to know why, Dean. You were so close to becoming a station agent, having your own band of operatives. Gable used to salivate when he spoke of you; that was what Olivier always said. You could have gone down in history."

"What history?"

"Our history. Our stamp on this planet."

"We are a plague."

"I am sorry that is how you view the Card. For then what has been the meaning of your life?"

"Nothing. There has been no meaning. I'm a locust."

"It's unfortunate that you aren't able to see all the good you've done, all the wishes you have fulfilled."

"Has the Card really fooled you into believing that? Your life is based on a lie, a facade. You are a machine not human–"

"That is your conscience taking over, whispering in your ear, allowing doubt to creep in. We are mini Gods, you and I; we are even more. We are capable of providing services that the almighty cannot even promise. With the kind of money the Card is accumulating, we can move mountains. And we're only getting started."

Marcus pushes the peanut to the front of his mouth and spits it out as hard as he can. The peanut spirals through the air, catching Omar directly in the eye. The operative loses his balance.

Marcus's Savate and Muy Thai training has made him equipped to use his feet as weapons. He lands a roundhouse kick to Omar's face, his toe clipping the guy in the same eye that the peanut just injured. The gun goes off but the bullet doesn't come close. Marcus is upon him, fists pummeling the guy's head, the Omar Sharif mask becoming deformed. He lands a final fist between Omar's eyes and sees blood dripping from the mask. He takes the gun from Omar and plants a bullet in the guy's neck, then slips the gun and his Kamikaze Knife into his waistband.

No one is around. No one has seen this.

He grabs his pack and heads back to the station just as the train to Seattle pulls in.

# 38

DURING THE SMOOTH TRAIN RIDE TO SEATTLE,
Marcus flirts with sleep but is unable to succumb even
though he craves it so. At least no surprise operatives
have been poised on the train to take him out. They
would be waiting at the airport instead. When Omar
Sharif fails to return with news of a kill, the airport will
become flooded. Marcus runs through his mind all the
possible operatives that could be sent: Jimmy Stewart,
Marlon Brando, Fred Astaire, Mae West, even Cagney,
plus all of the international operatives that are now
connected to this mission as well.

He arrives after midnight, the airport a giant glass
bubble. EVA Air is the only carrier that flies to Macau,
but he cautions himself not to go to that window first in
case someone is monitoring. After waiting in line at
three other windows without a sign of being followed,
he makes his way to EVA Air.

"One way ticket to Macau," he tells the small Asian
woman behind the desk. "When is the next flight?"

She types the info into her computer.

"Two hours," she says. "How will you be paying?"

This part might prove tricky, since paying in cash for an international flight often breeds scrutiny. He goes into a story about having a CD that finally matured and how it was easier to take it out in cash. The woman doesn't care, just asks for his passport and accepts the fat wad of cash.

"Any luggage to check?"

"No, I'll be carrying this on," he says, indicating his backpack.

"You will be boarding in an hour," she replies, handing him his pass.

An hour. He has two options. Either he can ditch the gun and knife and go through airport security now, or he could stay armed for as long as possible. He reasons that it's better to go through security before there's a chance he might be seen.

He leans over a garbage can, sticking the backpack all the way inside so he can dispose of the gun and the knife without any cameras seeing. He hears a clunk as they spill to the bottom, then he removes the backpack and zips it up.

On his way to security his heart drops, practically swims out of his mouth. On the escalator coming towards him is a lady who looks like Greta Garbo. He recognizes the umbrella-shaped eyebrows, the sad mouth, the drooping eyes, the exquisite beauty, except she's dressed in modern garb. She's fixated on him, those drooping eyes boring into his soul. She raises a hand in the pretend shape of a gun and pulls the fake trigger.

Since he never worked with Garbo before, she must be an international operative under Olivier's command like Omar. Even though Gable's operatives are often called to do international missions, Olivier's people are based in foreign hubs and often do the preliminary work while the operatives at the main office finish the job. Each international employee ultimately wants a promotion to the main office since it's a higher salary with less fluff jobs, or at least that's the propaganda that the Card spews.

As Garbo reaches the bottom of escalator, Marcus doubles back and walks swiftly until she's out of sight. He's too far away now from the garbage can where he threw out his weapons, no shot at getting them back. The airport is fairly empty at this time of night so she should be easy to spot but he doesn't see her anywhere.

Time is ticking down while he waits. He can't linger for too much longer before he needs to go through security. Garbo had seen him headed towards the S Gates, but thirteen different carriers go out of the S Gates so she wouldn't necessarily know he was flying EVA, unless she put two and two together and figured Rita or Omar Sharif spilled the beans about Gable's location.

After stalling a little longer, Marcus now has two options. He could leave the airport altogether, but then he will have lost the thousand dollars he used for the ticket to Macau. Even though he may throw Garbo off his tracks by doing so, there's also no guarantee that other operatives wouldn't get him the next time. He must chance it.

At a quick pace, he marches back to the S Gates security checkpoint. No sign of Garbo, but that doesn't mean she hasn't passed through. He's so nervous about catching sight of her that he has no time to worry about his fake passport and the small chance it could cause a problem. The TSA agent luckily waves him by and he complies with the song and dance of taking off his belt and shoes as he steps inside the X-ray scanner. They do a thorough check of him, no surprise because of the sketchy eye-patch, but soon he's let through and is on his way to the EVA air gate.

The majority of passengers waiting at the gate are of Asian descent. This relieves him at first until he wonders if Garbo could also be Asian underneath the mask as well. She had to have ditched the mask to get by security so he looks for anyone who comes off as suspicious. There's a tour of older Asian ladies, most of them conked out or talking on their cells. There's a man and his wife. A few non-Asians are milling about: a guy in a Hawaiian shirt, a businesswoman, and a girl in her twenties who looks to be a model.

He sits amongst the pack of older tourists, his foot tapping like crazy to the Debussy concerto *La Mer*— anything to calm him down. It isn't working. His stomach turns, sweat pours from his forehead. Thankfully a stewardess comes on the loud speaker and announces that they are ready to board.

His section is called last, most of the passengers having already boarded. He gives one last look at the airport, scanning for a trace of Garbo, but he doesn't see her. The stewardess takes his ticket and he's giddy as he heads through the tunnel, dumbfounded that he was able to elude the Card.

On the plane, the women on the tour are all seated up front. He checks his ticket and sees that it says 34C, an aisle seat.

When he reaches seat number 34, his body turns

into an ice block. All the blood rushes down and lands in his toes because next to him sits an older business-woman with her hair in a bun, the same one who'd been monitoring him at the Es Saadi Palace in Marrakesh. The same one who likely delivered the package full of Hasan Bouchtat's chopped-off fingers.

The airplane's doors have closed now and the stewardesses are all ordering him to sit.

He has no choice but to comply.

## 39

"Sit down," the businesswoman says, in a swedish accent just like Greta Garbo's. She is smiling a phony smile, ready for the show.

Marcus slowly eases into the seat. By the window is an old Asian woman. She greets him hello. He wonders if she's another operative or just one of the women from the tour. Her shirt says *Paradise Excursions,* with a palm tree growing out of the first S in *Excursions.* The O is an orange sun. It seems like Desire Card is just fucking with him, since paradise is his dream. He wonders if this tiny Asian woman with a cute face will be the one to do him in.

The old Asian woman says something in Cantonese he can't understand.

"She doesn't speak a lick of English," the business-woman replies. "So this is how it will go. Once we are in the air, I will slip you a pill. You will swallow this pill. You will have twenty minutes left to reflect on why this was done to you. These twenty minutes will be painful. Your organs will shut down one by one. You will have trouble breathing and in the end your heart will explode. That will be the last thing you feel."

"What if I won't let you do that?"

The businesswoman laughs.

"Then I will give this pill to the woman sitting next to me."

She looks over and smiles at the Asian woman who is looking out the window, delighted as the plane begins to roll down the runway.

"Is this how Gable told you to play this?" he asks.

"Pretty much, I improvised a little."

She takes the old woman's hand.

"You're gonna die," she tells her, smiling wider than before, an exaggerated cartoon.

"*Thank you*," the old woman replies in Cantonese.

The captain comes on the speakers and says they're ready for takeoff.

Marcus tells himself that he will be getting off this plane in Macau and the businesswoman with a bun in her hair will not. There is no other outcome that could occur after all he's been through. And the old woman will survive too.

The plane begins its ascent, the takeoff rocky at first, wheels squealing, bags from the overhead compartment falling over, the women on the tour yelling. Finally, the plane finds it groove and flies into dark clouds. The tiny lights of Seattle blink below and then disappear entirely.

"We have three dead operatives because of you," the businesswoman says. "In a span of days, you have caused us to lose millions of dollars. All because of your ignorance."

She takes out a vial full of pink pills. They look like

Tic-Tacs. She removes one pill and holds it in her palm.

"Swallow it whole. Go out with a sliver of dignity."

The seatbelt light pops off.

"Go fuck yourself," he says, grabbing her vial of pills instead and jumping out of his seat. He flies down the aisle, knocking a stewardess to the side, and heads into a bathroom. He locks the door and flushes the stash of pills. *Okay*, he thinks, catching his breath. *What's next? What's fucking next?*

He hears the bathroom lock being toyed with. All of a sudden it switches from occupied to vacant. He tries to block the door, but the businesswoman is too strong. She bursts inside, the bun in her hair unraveled, a good forty inches spilling from her head.

"You fucking coward," she says, as the two wrestle around in the cramped space. The sink turns on, the toilet flushes. She slams his face into the mirror and wraps her long hair around his neck twice, tight enough to choke him. He lets out a wet cough, struggling to breathe as she tightens the vice. She pries his mouth open and stuffs her last pink pill under his tongue. She clamps his mouth down but the pill is protected by his tongue and stays intact. He stops trying to fight her, pretending to give up. She's still squeezing his neck, a sadistic grin taking over her face. He opens his mouth and points to show her that the pill is gone.

"Little baby swallowed it like a good boy?" she asks, loosening her grip, enough for him to swivel around and lunge at her with his mouth. Their teeth collide as he shoves his tongue down her throat, the pill dislodged and on its way into her stomach. He keeps kissing her, just to make sure, her tongue already tasting like death, coppery like licking an old penny.

When he pulls away, she is no longer the confident operative who thought she had won this war: her face betrays her, ages a decade in seconds. He realizes she might try to throw up the pill so he puts his hand over her mouth. She tries to gag, but he doesn't relent. She waves her hands in the air for him to stop. Finally, he removes his hand.

"It's in my system already," she says. "There's nothing to do. I can only wait."

Since he can't trust that she won't attack again, he puts pressure on the back of her neck until she faints. He leaves the bathroom holding her up. No one notices since the lights are out and the passengers in the back are sleeping. He brings her back to their seats. The old Asian woman is sleeping as well, her light snores the sweetest thing he's heard in some time.

He positions the businesswoman in her seat. She begins to stir a little bit and her sad eyes open.

"I had two pills left," she manages to say through heavy breaths.

"What?"

A smile curls up her face.

"I told you I would kill her if you didn't take your pill."

Her eyes shift over to the old Asian woman.

"Why?" he says, practically in tears. "What purpose does her death serve?"

"Because we don't make empty threats at the Desire Card, and you're a fool if you haven't figured this out yet. We will end you."

"You can keep trying—"

"It is not about trying, it is an absolute."

She reaches into her giant purse and removes the

Greta Garbo mask. With a mirror in hand, she fixes the hair until only perfection stares back.

"You killed her," Greta Garbo says, nodding at the old Asian woman. "Just remember that."

She clutches her stomach in pain, the mask's mouth somehow twisting into what looks like a frown. Then he hears a tiny pop coming from her body and imagines her heart has exploded. A few seconds later, a tiny pop comes from the old Asian woman too.

"Fuck," he says, his face red and full of tears. All he can say is "fuck" over and over, there's nothing else left in him.

Finally, he composes himself because this will get him nowhere. There is still too much left to do to survive. He wants to sleep more than anything, but he swore not to do that until he gets to Macau, just in case Gable had one more surprise up his sleeve thirty thousand feet in the air.

So he turns on the reading light. His hands are shaking while he reaches into his backpack for *The Call of the Wild*, his Bible to keep him awake and grounded. He fixates on a highlighted passage bookmarked by Gramps' photo.

*"Here was neither peace, nor rest, nor a moment's safety. All was confusion and action, and every moment life and limb were in peril. There was an imperative need to be constantly alert...for they were savages, all of them."*

He reads it again and again and again, endlessly, until it's tattooed in his brain and the plane is making its descent into Macau.

# 40

THE MOMENT MARCUS SEES THE GLITZY LIGHTS OF Macau winking along the horizon, he grabs his backpack and heads to the front of the plane. He needs to be one of the first passengers off so he can avoid the fallout from the two dead people in the seats next to him. When the plane lands, he's out of the door before he hears any hubbub from the rear. Customs is the next hurdle, since he's traveling without luggage and holding a shit ton of cash. Luckily, the thrill of Macau's casinos is enough of an excuse. The last stop is to exchange some of his cash for *pataca*.

He exits the airport that is situated on a slim island shaped like a mini Manhattan. The air is humid, a reprieve from the bitter cold of the last few weeks. He hops in a cab, telling the driver in Cantonese to take him to the largest hotel for the best price. He winds up at the Zhuhai Charming Holiday, a towering monstrosity where he won't stand out. At the front desk, he pays for a room for the next three days and warns the girl that he wants privacy and doesn't need maid service during his stay. Even though three days is a short timeframe to find Gable's son, if he stays any longer he won't have any cash left to get to Fiji.

Upstairs he eyes the queen-sized bed, lustfully falls into the sheets. Strips off his clothes and allows himself this long-awaited sleep, curling up into the fetal position with the caress of the pillow against his cheek. His dream takes him into another realm. A wrought-iron gate opening its jaws wide as J.D. enters a party surrounded by flames. In this world, he hasn't fully become Marcus Edmonton yet. Most of the guests are other operatives: Jimmy Stewart and Cary Grant talking over cigars. Marlon Brando and Fred Astaire sharing a bottle of Scotch. Gary Cooper flirting with a dolled-up Mae West. The guests up front are the ones he has already killed. Bogart with his hangdog face, a cool cigarette in hand. He's clutching Rita Hayworth close, dancing a wild dance to the beat of bongo drums.

"We've been waiting for you," Bogart says, tipping his fedora.

Rita's got a bullet hole between her eyes. Its leaking blood but she mops it up with a handkerchief.

"I call it my third eye now thanks to you," she says. "It saw that you will be joining us soon."

Omar Sharif and Greta Garbo share a blood-red drink in the corner. They raise their glasses to him with a frown.

The Twins are there as well, sampling a platter of deviled eggs. They stop chewing at the same time to give him the finger.

Abram dances in the center of it all, his body flailing around like he's having a seizure. Only the whites of his eyes are showing and his body contours in ways that aren't physically possible, limbs twisting in directions they've never twisted before. Keeping to the beat, he comes closer, the whites of his eyes filled with bloodshot veins.

"You motherfucker. Did ya have to plug me in the stomach?"

He's still moving to the beat, the thump of the drums getting faster.

"You were gonna kill me, Abram."

"Yeah, I was gonna kill ya, but fuck, man."

"I had to get you first. I have to get all of you first."

"She will be joining us soon as well," Abram says, his crooked index finger wagging back and forth.

"Who?"

"Annie of course," Abram says, laughing as he dances away into the flames.

"Where am I?" J.D. asks, his voice smaller than ever.

James Cagney appears from out of a puff of smoke, the smell rancid and unforgiving. He has the angriest mug of them all.

"I think you know," Cagney says. Spit flying from his mouth. "So why fight it if this is where you're bound to wind up anyway, with all of us, dancing for eternity."

The bongo drums get louder and louder, a drill in J.D.'s ear.

"The only reason you're still alive is that you haven't encountered me yet during this excursion," Cagney says, a grin creeping up his cheek. "But now that will change, you dirty rat. That other eye of yours is mine."

Cagney bears his fangs and digs his nails into J.D.'s left eye, ripping it out.

J.D. can't see anything anymore, the party a dark void, the smell of fire stronger than ever.

"Come," James Cagney says, taking him by the hand. "The Boss is ready for you."

He is led beyond the flames into a room off to the side. A door shuts.

"Cagney?" he calls out. "Cagney?!"

"He is gone," a deep robotic voice replies, sounding like it's coming from all sides of the room.

"Gable..."

"I have to say I never thought you'd make it this far, Dean. I knew I considered you one of my best for a reason."

"This is just a dream," he whispers.

"No, this is the future," Gable responds. "One that I can assure you will occur. You and I in a dark room together, a knife between us sealing your fate."

Gable removes a knife from its holder, the blade singing.

"A future where I gut you good."

He can feel Gable's breath in front of him, a stinking cloud. They are standing close enough to kiss. J.D. swings his arms to fight, but no one is there.

Suddenly, the knife is plunged into his gut. Gable pulls the knife out and shoves it back in, over and over, unrelenting, until J.D.'s organs spool from his body and sizzle on the hot floor.

"There will be a feast tonight with you as the main course," Gable cries. "But that heart of yours is just for me."

Gable stabs the knife into J.D.'s chest and cuts out the heart, holding it beating in his fist.

J.D. can hear Gable devouring his heart, lips smacking and a satisfied belch once it is finished.

He collapses to the floor, his face down in a puddle of organs.

Finally, Gable ends it all by giving a quick stomp to his head and turning the darkness into death.

## 41

A SOUL-WRENCHING PANIC ATTACK GRIPS MARCUS as he shoots out of bed, the nightmarish dream still a part of him. Thankfully, his heart is still intact in his chest. It's nighttime and he's slept for a full day, not ideal but obviously necessary, even though he doesn't feel rested at all. He takes a long overdue shower, the pulse of the water a godsend. Days of dirt spiraling down the drain. Once he finishes up, the dream becomes a memory, no longer a prophesied future. Time to plan his next step.

With half a million people on eleven square miles, Macau isn't the best place for Gable's son to hide, especially if he's an albino. It's not worth searching the casinos because there are too many. It's also not likely the son would go gambling since a big win might mean a ticket home to jail. If the son's life back home consisted of getting fucked up at gay clubs like Rita said, then Marcus's best shot is to troll any gay establishments here.

He goes down to the lobby and checks the Internet to find only one gay club mentioned – Destination Bar.

————

He heads to Destination Bar on foot, wanting to get a feel for the city. He's traveled to other places in China on missions before, comfortable with the customs and capable of a basic conversation in Cantonese. On a Friday night, Macau's streets are busy and alive. Neon lights and tall glass skyscrapers. A Vegas of the East, except while people head to Vegas for entertainment, they come to Macau to invest. Precisely why Gable has circled the area for years to build a new casino. To the Boss's credit, he's never entered into a bad business venture before.

Destination Bar is located off of a main thoroughfare. He scopes it out for a half an hour but doesn't see anyone entering except for a lanky Asian guy. When he goes inside, pop music blasts from the speakers while a strobe light illuminates a few men pawing at each other on the dance floor and a go-go dancer working the stage. Mostly Chinese clientele; he's the only Caucasian there. He sits at the bar with a good view of the entrance and motions for the bartender to come closer.

"Speak English?" Marcus asks. "My Cantonese is limited."

The bartender nods. He has long eyelashes and big eyes like a porcelain doll.

"Are there any other gay bars in Macau?"

"The government shut the rest down," the bartender says, with his hand on his hip. "Destination Bar is now the only destination."

"Good, I'll take a Scotch. Neat."

The bartender pours and Marcus relishes the first sip of a Balvenie Doublewood. It's been some time since he's gotten the chance to enjoy a Scotch. He finishes it rather quickly and orders another. This time he'll drink it more slowly; make it last through the night.

———

Two hours and three Scotches later, most would be pleasantly snookered, but Marcus has always been able to hold his own. Maybe that's just a sign of an alcoholic? He doesn't know how he could be anything else after all he's been through.

Just as he's ready to order another, he spies a middle-aged white man entering the bar. The man has a paunch, pasty skin, and very white hair styled with an abundance of product. Hard to tell if he's a true albino or not. However, if this isn't Gable's son, then the guy definitely has a doppelganger in Macau.

The white-haired man eyes Marcus and sits at the end of the bar. He gives an awkward smile that makes him look constipated and calls the bartender over with a curl of his finger. The bartender pours two drinks and hands one to Marcus.

"This is a gift from him," the bartender says, batting his long eyelashes at the white-haired man.

The white-haired man gives a too-da-loo wave and slides over.

"Now I've been coming to this place since I arrived in Macau, but I have yet to come across someone like you," the man says, gnawing at the straw in his drink.

Marcus has never flirted with a guy before, but he

knows he's successful in the art of manipulation. So he turns on the charm.

"I could say the same," he says, winking with his good eye.

"I'm Chip."

"Marcus."

They shake hands. Chip's is cold and clammy, his fingers plump like Vienna sausages.

"*A shante*, Marcus. And that eye-patch of yours...so mysterious. What brings you to Macau?"

"Business. My firm is investing in a casino being built here."

He watches Chip carefully to see if he offers any type of reaction. The guy is high on something, his eyes glassy, pupils dilated; but Chip is good at holding his cards close to his chest as well. No apparent sign of this story resonating at all.

"Ooooh, a big shot businessman. Making deals. Making money."

"And what brings you here?"

"Oh *moi*? I'm...taking a break from the States."

Now Chip reveals himself, the words said with a sad undertone.

"Another drink?" Marcus asks, pointing at Chip's empty glass.

"You're gonna get me snookered."

"Isn't that the point?" Marcus replies, knocking back his own Scotch and waving the bartender over for two more.

————

A few drinks later, Chip is wasted while Marcus is still tight.

"Well, I don't really work," Chip says, hugging his drink close to his chest like it's a tiny kitten. "I mean my family is very wealthy. I mean more money than you can imagine. Like there are tiny countries with a smaller per capita income. Anyway, my father helped me set up this PR firm in Greenwich, Connecticut, but I let my underlings run the day-to-day minutiae. It's called Chipper PR. Celebrity events in the Tri-State. You know it?"

"What does your family do?"

"Mother comes from old money, but my father has many businesses. He's actually here to build a casino."

Chip sticks his tongue in the glass to lick at the last drops.

"What's his casino called?"

Chip puts his hand on Marcus's knee, practically has to hold on to stay upright.

"Why don't you come back to my hotel and I could tell you more about it in private?"

Marcus places his hand over Chip's. He's so close to Gable now, possibly moments away. His stomach is doing flips.

"Lead the fucking way, Chipper," he smiles.

"Pinch me, cause I think I'm dreaming," Chip purrs.

# 42

CHIP'S PENTHOUSE SUITE IS IN A HIGH-END HOTEL overlooking Macau's glittering skyscrape. The plan is to get in, get the info about Gable's whereabouts, and get the fuck out. Marcus is at the window admiring the stunning views when he hears Chip lock the door. All of a sudden, he feels uncertain. Chip could be an operative after all, luring him into a trap. Another operative could be waiting behind the curtain with a silencer. He knows this because he's been that other operative.

He moves the curtain aside.

"Peek-a-boo," Chip giggles, goosing him from behind.

The room is dark, only the neon lights from outside illuminating Chip's doughy face.

Marcus takes a step back, keeping as much of a distance as possible.

"Is your father staying at this hotel too?"

Chip doesn't respond, more interested in pulling out a glass pipe filled with shards of crystals.

"I have some delicious stuff," Chip says, taking a hit. "It'll keep us going all night."

He holds out the pipe, its stench criminal. Marcus shakes his head.

Chip shrugs his shoulders and takes another puff.

"So does your father stay with you here?" Marcus asks, more forceful this time.

"I don't want to talk about my father," Chip groans. "He's a son-of-a-bitch. I want to get dirty."

Marcus has had enough of this. Time to get answers.

"Do you like to get tied up?" Marcus asks.

"If you could read my mind, Pirate."

Chip giggles and strips down to his underwear, the sight of his flabby body startling.

"Get on the bed," Marcus orders.

Chip lies on his back and gives a pose.

"You like what you see, Mr. Stud?"

Marcus collects the bed sheets and ties Chip's hands to the bedpost and his feet to the footboard.

"There are toys in the top drawer over there if you're so inclined," Chip says.

Marcus opens the drawer and finds various flagellation devices. He chooses a painful looking whip.

"Ooooh, my naughty eye-patch man. Now you be easy on me, nothing that will leave any major scars."

"That's not how this is gonna work."

He whips Chip across the chest as hard as he can, drawing blood.

"Not so hard," Chip screams. "Are you insane?"

"Close to it."

He wipes the blood off the whip, sees the fear reflected in Chip's eyes.

"I want information, Chipper. That's all. If you give me what I want, I won't hurt you like that again. But if you don't, I know every torture method in the book."

"W-what do you want to know?"

"I need you to tell me about your father."

Chip scrunches up his face. "My father? What the *fuck*? What is happening? What kind of shit did I just smoke?"

Marcus whips him again, harder this time. A bloody X now carved into Chip's chest.

Chip lets out a deafening scream. This one rattles the walls.

"Stop screaming or I'll pull out your tongue," he says, covering Chip's mouth. "Do you hear me?"

Chip nods with a whimper so Marcus removes his hand.

"Now what do you know about the Desire Card?"

"The what? I-I-I don't even know what you're talking about."

"The Desire Card! The fucking Desire Card!"

Out of frustration, Marcus whips Chip across the face. A welt opens up on the guy's forehead and runs down to his chin, almost in the shape of a question mark. For a second, Marcus is taken back to his battle with Bogart at the cottage in Vermont. He had just plugged Bogart in the chest and removed the guy's mask to discover a face with a similar shaped scar.

The whip has become independent from his hand, its own animal.

"Okay, okay," Chip cries, his face a mix of blood, flesh, and gobs of tears. "I'll tell you whatever you want. Just no more. Please, no more."

Marcus slows down the whipping, finally stops. He's out of breath once he does, his head spinning.

"My father...is a business tycoon," Chip says, a dying sob between each breath. "Self-made. The type... with his hands in a lot of cookie jars."

"And this casino he's building. What's it called?"

"The Excelsior... It'll be the tallest in the world once it's finished... Some Moroccan guy got a permit to build an even bigger one... My father is here to...deal with that."

"Does that mean he's here to kill him? Does this have anything to do with the Desire Card?"

Chip shakes his head. "Kill him? What? I don't...no, no, it's a business thing."

Marcus whips him across the face again.

"I swear," Chip yells, spitting out a tooth. "Oooh, my tooth," he whines. "I HAVE NEVER HEARD OF THE DESIRE CARD. I am not lying, I'm not! My father has a ton of businesses that I don't know about. He...we were never close. He...never wanted to have anything to do with me, okay? O-Fucking-Kay?"

"Is he staying at this hotel, too?"

"No, this would be...low class for him. He's at the Four Seasons."

"What name is he staying under?"

"Excelsior...like the casino."

"Do you have a picture of him?"

Chip points to a drawer.

Inside Marcus finds a framed photograph of Chip's family. He takes the picture out of its frame. Smiles and eggnogs in everyone's hands. A mountain of presents underneath a Christmas tree that's two stories high.

Chip and his elegant mother, arm-in-arm. A pretty middle-aged daughter to their left, a younger version of the mother. Her sad sack husband next to her, looking like he wants to be anywhere else. Two grandchildren up front, a teenage boy and a little girl in her school uniform.

There is a cigarette burn in place of Gable's face.

"Someone burned a hole in your father's face."

"Oh yeah...forgot...I was pissed at him yesterday. I know he has plans to...leave me here, write me off...."

Chip keeps babbling but Marcus isn't listening. He pockets the picture and picks up a pillow. Chip's eyes go wide.

"Oh shit, what are you gonna do?"

Marcus doesn't answer.

"What are you gonna fucking do, you psychopath? Please don't kill me, please don't kill me. I won't say *anything* to my father. Whatever business you have with him has nothing to do with me. I never saw you. I swear, I...I never saw you."

Marcus takes off the pillowcase and stuffs it in Chip's mouth.

Chip tries to gag but the pillowcase is stuffed too deep.

Marcus places the pillow over Chip's face. He has to kill this man. To keep him alive leaves the opportunity open for Gable to be contacted. Marcus's only chance is to have the element of surprise on his side. He pushes the pillow down.

Chip writhes around, screaming with all his might through the gag and the pillow.

Marcus presses harder, putting his knee up on the bed for leverage.

Chip is desperately trying to free himself but the bed sheets are tied too tight.

And then, seemingly out of nowhere, Marcus thinks of the old Asian woman from the plane. He sees her delighted expression as the plane took off and then her blank stare once her heart exploded. He hears Garbo telling him that he's responsible.

There has to be some type of code that he maintains, otherwise why did he decide to leave the Card at all? Refusing to kill Hasan Bouchtat cannot mean that a trail of innocent people would be dead in his place. The Twins and Abram were one thing, bad to the core, bound to be responsible for a lot of bloodshed in their lives. And while survival is still paramount, while that has always been ingrained in him, there has to be a purpose for this last seven years of hell, for this past week of carnage: to ultimately rid the world of the Desire Card once and for all by capturing its king, and wiping out any operatives who get in the way. But Chip is not an operative. And while the guy probably should be in prison for what he did back in the States, Marcus isn't here to play lawmaker. Nor is he solely an executioner. He won't be responsible for another innocent life.

He releases the pillow as Chip gasps for air. He removes another pillowcase and ties it around Chip's mouth and jaw with a Constrictor knot, just like Gramps had taught him to do as a kid, impossible to untie when tightened.

"You're welcome," he says, leaving Chip squirming.

He exits the room and flips the sign on the doorknob to Do Not Disturb.

# 43

AT THE CRACK OF DAWN THE NEXT MORNING, Marcus goes to the lobby of the Four Seasons. The hotel is grand and palatial with tall columns, flowing staircases, and marbled floors. In the center, a giant bouquet in the shape of a dragon's head breathes a fire of red lotus flowers. There's just a smattering of people, mostly Chinese businessman. He verifies at the front desk that a guest is staying under the name Excelsior, but they wouldn't give him the room number. Better to stalk Gable from the lobby and follow him to where the casino is being built. So he sits on a couch with his back to the main elevator bank, a mirror to the left giving him a full view.

He takes out the family picture he stole from Chip and runs his finger across the burned hole where Gable's head should be.

The morning stretches on, his back beginning to ache, no sign of Gable or any other operatives. A guy at the front desk starting to give him a look. Marcus has a steak knife in his waistband from ordering room service at his hotel last night. It seems like the guy is looking right at it. He hates that for the rest of his life he has to be suspicious of everyone.

*Ding.*

The elevator next to the front desk opens and a woman steps out in a chic blue blouse with white pants. She has a cream-colored scarf wrapped around her head and big black sunglasses. A peek of blond hair spills out of the scarf, not bottle-blond, but real blond. A dot of red lipstick and an upturned nose.

Annie.

His legs go weak. If he were standing up, he would've fallen over. He shakes his head, deeming it a hallucination. He has the urge to run to her, doesn't know what he'd do once she'd see him. He tells himself to stay in place. He physically has to hold his legs down. He knows he'll want to kiss her when he probably should stab. The fact that she's here means she's being used as bait.

She walks briskly to the entrance, high heels clomping against the marble. He's never seen her in high heels before. This is a different girl than the one he thought he knew.

He pockets the photo of Gable's family and follows her out the door.

Outside she walks up to a black car waiting at the curb. She looks to the left and the right, then gets inside.

Marcus pops into a taxi idling two cars away.

"Follow that black car," Marcus says in Cantonese.

The driver turns around. Shakes his head no.

"Do it," Marcus says, pulling out a stack of *pataca*.

"*Hǎo*," the driver says, all smiles now.

The driver waits a moment after the black car

leaves before taking off. Like a good stalker, he makes sure to remain two cars behind. The traffic on the streets is intense, the roads clogged with trishaws and buses.

Marcus can see the back of Annie's head in the black car. She's sitting next to a man, but he can't see the guy's face. There's a possibility that she could've been working for the Card all along. He can't rule that out as much as he might want to. She could be the up-and-coming Mae West he's heard so much about at the main office. It was naïve to think that Gable didn't know Annie was a part of Marcus's past. Gable had probably combed through all the people left in his life and employed each one as a trainee. Annie could've already been contacted before he went to Marrakesh, for Gable always liked being one step ahead.

But it couldn't be. Annie had plenty of chances to kill him, unless at some point she actually fell in love and couldn't go through with it. Couldn't even let Rita do the deed.

Whatever she's involved with here, he won't forget that Annie still saved his life back in Killenroy.

Finally, the black car pulls up to a casino that reaches into the clouds. The entire building made of dark glass. The word Excelsior brandished with golden lights.

Marcus tells the driver to stop, a few yards away.

Annie steps out with the man who takes her arm. Marcus's depth perception makes it hard to tell if the man took her arm forcefully or out of politeness. The man's face is ghoulish, covered with what looks like acid burns. The Scream painting brought to life. He's dressed in khakis, a buttoned-up shirt and a wool jacket.

The Man with Acid Burns whisks Annie into the casino.

Marcus gets out of the taxi, heads inside the casino as well. Gable's lobby putting the Four Seasons to shame. Opulent and exotic. Velvet chairs. Sparkling chandeliers. Mirrors upon mirrors. An even grander floral arrangement: The Great Wall of China made up of white roses.

He sees an elevator door close. He watches it climb to the fiftieth floor and stop. He takes another elevator up to the same floor, steps out into a hallway. It's dark except for a few lanterns casting a dim light. He walks down the hallway without making a sound, has to train his ear to pick up the slightest movement. To his left and right are empty rooms filled with casino equipment. At the end, there's an open room. He goes inside to find Annie tied to a chair by her cream-colored scarf.

He reaches for the steak knife should he need it, his fingers millimeters away.

# 44

"J.D.?" Annie says, a tear dripping from her sunglasses. "Oh J.D., you gotta help me. These people..."

She's shivering, not from cold, from fear.

Marcus puts a finger to his lips. "Keep quiet."

The room is unfinished, no other furniture besides the chair. No place for the Man with Acid Burns to hide.

He takes out the steak knife, holds it to her neck. "All right, talk. What are you doing here? And don't lie to me."

"J.D., who are these people? You don't know what they said they'd do to me."

"Did they get to you before I even showed up in Killenroy?"

"What? No...it was after you left. While I was figuring out what to do with Carmen...I mean Rita's body, a man came to my door looking for you..."

"I want to see your eyes."

"What? My eyes?"

He takes off her sunglasses.

"Look at me and tell me this is the truth."

"J.D., of course it's the truth. I don't know who these people are. When the man came to my door, it looked like his face was dipped in boiling acid like some comic book villain. Like the Joker. He said that Rita had contacted him 'bout the two of us, me and you, that we were shacking up. When he didn't hear from Rita in over a day, he came looking and found her rental car by my front yard."

Marcus watches her eyes carefully, searches for any tell that proves she's lying: a micro-expression that reveals her true emotion, or if her eyes move to the right at all.

"He had a gun to my head and said he'd shoot me if I didn't tell him where you went. Told me my name is Annie Duluth and my family lives in Coldstream, Kentucky. Said they have someone there who's just waiting for him to give the signal to slit my parents' throats. He even described what their house looked like, white with black shutters."

Her eyes look to the left the entire time, exactly what right-handed people do when they're trying to remember something, not lying.

"Are you right handed?" he asks.

"Am I what?"

"Right handed, Annie? Are you right handed?"

"Yeah, yeah I am. Why do you want to know?"

"Forget it. Do they know that I'm here right now?"

"You mean in Macau?"

"I mean in this building."

"No...I don't think so. Well, I've seen some cameras along the walls so they might know now, but that man didn't say nothin' about you in the car. He was taking me to his boss, but then in the elevator he got some call on this weird-lookin' headset. Brought me to this room and tied me up."

"Where did he go?"

"I don't know, but I heard the stairway door close so he must've taken that."

Marcus heads toward the door.

"Wait, J.D., you're gonna leave me all tied up? J.D., I told you the truth."

"The jury's still out on that," he calls back.

He's already in the hallway before she can respond. Whether she was telling the truth or not, she was brought here to distract him but he won't let her be his downfall. He runs into the stairwell, looks one floor down and one floor up. The exit door one floor up is ajar.

Knife in hand, he climbs the stairs and peeps through the crack. The hallway is dark just like the floor below, a few lanterns glowing orange and casting shadows on a man in a suit, the guy's back facing the door. The man turns to reveal his profile.

Cary Grant.

Marcus eases the door open. The tiniest creak echoes through the hallway, sounding like a mouse's squeak.

Cary Grant swivels around to Marcus jamming the steak knife into his throat. Blood spews, an open geyser. Like a busted doll, Cary Grant collapses into Marcus's arms.

He swipes Grant's gun, checks to see how many bullets it has left. Luckily, it's got a full barrel.

"Where is he?" Marcus asks, pressing the knife further into the guy's throat.

Cary Grant points a quivering finger toward a door at the end.

He lets go of Grant's body and creeps down the hallway until he's inches from the door.

In the room, the Man with Acid Burns has a gun pointed at someone with a bag over their head. The person is on their knees.

Two quick shots are fired.

The person with the bag over their head slumps to the floor.

Marcus hiccups, the sound from out of nowhere.

The Man with Acid Burns hears the hiccup, his face tilting towards the source.

Marcus has no other choice but to charge inside, gun blazing.

# 45

MARCUS TAKES ONE SHOT AND CLIPS THE MAN WITH Acid Burns in his upper right arm. He misses the brachial artery on purpose, wanting to keep the guy alive. The Man with Acid Burns gets a shot off as well, the bullet lodged in the ceiling. Marcus kicks the gun away, pulls the guy up by his collar.

"Where is Gable?"

He sticks his gun in the Man with Acid Burns' chest, a bullet ready for the guy's heart.

"Ah, fuck, Dean," the Man with Acid Burns cries, clamping a hand over the wound.

"Do we know each other? Have we worked together before?"

The Man with Acid Burns looks at Marcus with puppy dog eyes. He gives an *aww shucks* half smile.

"In the whole vast configuration of things, I'd say you were nothing but a scurvy spider," the Man with Acid Burns says, his voice quaky with an exaggerated mid-Atlantic accent.

"That's from *It's a Wonderful Life*. Jimmy Stewart?"

"Remember that mission we did together to the Yukon?" Jimmy Stewart says, his voice quaking even more. "We were after that Russian ex-spy who'd been hiding away there for years."

"Two weeks of freezing my nuts off."

"But you were the one who found him, Dean. Off a tip from some drunk Inuit. It was pitch black out that night, but you sensed the Russian was close, located his hideout. Shot him in the right arm just where you shot me. So he wouldn't die and we could take him back to the client who'd been waiting for this guy since the 1980s."

"Boris Kazinksy."

"One of the top KGB agents during the Cold War, an old man still built like a brick house. Boris had been living off hunting moose."

"And then the client tortured and killed him?"

"Most likely, yes. But we are not in a business of judgments."

"I am no longer in this business."

Jimmy Stewart laughs but the laughter turns into a coughing attack, dots of blood spraying from his mouth.

"This...business we are in, Dean. It is who we are."

"It's who *you* are," Marcus says, getting red in the face, getting angry. Itching to squeeze the trigger.

"The man you were when you joined us...J.D. Storm...he no longer exists," Jimmy Stewart says.

"I am fucking aware of that. I'm someone new."

"You don't get to do that."

"I've changed my passport and I have a new name. I

will kill Gable and forget that the Card ever existed. I will live each day like it could be my last. And I'll be good. I'll do good things, I'll help people. I'll be someone, truly someone."

"You won't kill Gable. He knows you're here right now. He's already two steps ahead. And this noble crusade you are on is meaningless."

Jimmy Stewart glances over at the dead person with the bag over their head.

"Take the bag off his head."

A panic begins at the top of Marcus's spine, the tips of his fingers going numb.

"Who is that?"

"Take the bag off his head and find out."

"Is this some kind of trick?"

A line of blood spills from the person's head, no chance he's alive.

Marcus keeps the gun trained on Jimmy Stewart while he removes the bloody bag from the person's head.

Staring back with a cold, dead gaze is Hasan Bouchtat—the mark he refused to kill in Morocco.

Marcus almost loses his grip on the gun, the sight of a dead Hasan Bouchtat overwhelming. He feels the shock in temples, in his stomach that turns. He looks over at the body and notices that all the fingers are still intact.

"Whose fingers were sent to my hotel room in Marrakesh?"

Jimmy Stewart laughs again, even though it's obviously painful to do so.

"After you failed to ice the mark, he took off.

Vanished. But he left his wife and kids behind like they all do in the end. Fred Astaire and Marlon Brando came to the house. They chopped off the wife's fingers, found a couple of his rings lying around, then had them sent to your hotel as a message."

"You people are insane."

"You are the insane one! The wife bled out, she is dead now. If you killed the mark like you were supposed to, she would be alive. Do you understand that? Your mistake cost that woman her life. And now Gable is gonna make sure there will be a pile of bodies on your conscience."

"What about the two kids?"

"We left the kids alive. Their death served no purpose then."

"None of these deaths serve a purpose. We...you are a glorified hitman, nothing more. Whatever nonsense Gable has filled your head with, that's all it is... nonsense. You kill because someone pays top dollar. How much was Hasan's head?"

"A billion," Jimmy Stewart replies.

"A billion?"

"The mark was the top investor for The Excelsior, but he was trying to play Gable the whole time. He'd been planning on building another casino that would be a few stories taller and block the view."

"So there was no client that wished for Hasan's death?"

"Gable was the client. Not the first time he'd been one either." Jimmy Stewart pauses to wipe the blood from his mouth so he can continue speaking. "Gable has had suspicions about you for a while, ever since you hesitated with the girl in New York City outside of the club. He didn't want the mark dead in Marrakesh, just wanted him spooked. He knew that the mark would run to Macau to finalize plans for his precious casino. And then, in one of his most brilliant acts yet, Gable found a purpose for the mark's kids. Dangled them out of a window until the mark signed the papers to cancel all construction of his casino permanently. Not even his death could promise that."

"Did Gable drop those kids?"

Jimmy Stewart shrugs his shoulders, winces from the pain.

"You fucking freak," Marcus yells, choking Jimmy Stewart with his free hand, his thumb jammed in the guy's windpipe. "You're all fucking freaks."

Jimmy Stewart gasps for air.

Marcus staggers back, points the gun at Jimmy Stewart's other arm and aims for the brachial artery this time. Fires a shot.

"What about Annie?"

Jimmy Stewart lets out a death howl, the bullet stuck in his shoulder.

"What about Annie?" Marcus screams. "Was she in on this, too?"

Jimmy Stewart coughs up a dollop of blood, his body starting to shake.

"Was she conning me all along?" Marcus cries. "Did she tell you where we had planned to go?"

White pus pours from Jimmy Stewart's mouth, a dog gone rabid.

"When did Gable employ her? How long does this go back?"

Jimmy Stewart motions for Marcus to come closer.

Marcus leans down, sweat pooling from his head,

afraid of what he's about to hear. But he needs to know whether he can burn down this entire place, or if Annie's worth saving.

"There's not much I can tell you about this war," Jimmy Stewart says, the quaky mid-Atlantic accent still pitch-perfect. "It's like all wars, I guess. The undertakers are winning."

Marcus recognizes the speech. Jimmy Stewart gave the same one in the movie *Shenandoah* at the site of his wife's grave after most of his family was killed.

Marcus knows it's futile to ask about Annie anymore, for Jimmy Stewart is dead.

———

He trudges down a flight of stairs, a gun in each hand, ready to find out for once and for all if Annie's telling the truth. He reasons he must do whatever it takes until he's certain. But when he reaches the room where she was tied up, all that remains are the chair and her cream-colored scarf.

The word *PENTHOUSE* is written on the scarf in fresh blood.

The door to the stairwell slams.

He rushes out in the hallway and bolts through the exit door. He hears the sound of footsteps running up the stairs, two stories higher. He takes the stairs two at a time, trying to gain distance on whoever is running away from him.

The exit door opens one floor up. Seconds later, Marcus bursts through the door as well, practically stumbles into the hallway. The ding of an elevator resounds and he sees that one has opened to his left. He leaps to catch the doors in time before they close, manages to stop them. The gun in his hand goes off as the elevator opens and he flings himself inside.

James Cagney greets him with a brass-knuckle punch to his face.

## 46

THE BRASS-KNUCKLES PUNCH BREAKS MARCUS'S nose. Blood leaks from his nostrils, feeling like lava. Both his guns spiral to the floor, too far away to grab. He raises his fists in defense but James Cagney follows with a right uppercut, then a left uppercut. Gives Marcus a second to settle before a left hook knocks him to the floor.

"Get up. Get up you son-of-a-bitch."

James Cagney stands over him, his face looking like a mean bulldog. His body is stocky but solid, just like the movie star.

Marcus's good eye starts to swell from the uppercut, Cagney going in and out of focus.

Cagney grabs Marcus's neck and pulls him to his feet. Slams him into the wall as the elevator shakes around.

"You double-crossing dirty rat."

Cagney swings, a quick jab to Marcus's jaw.

Marcus clamps down on his tongue, the taste of

blood in his teeth. He staggers backwards, trying to get his footing so he can locate where the guns fell.

"Do you know the amount of damage your little stunt has caused so far?" Cagney yells. He pops Marcus in the stomach, grinding the brass knuckles into Marcus's belly.

Marcus hits the floor hard, the pain shooting up his back. He pushes through it. Gets down even lower and lunges for Cagney's leg. Sinks his teeth in. He sees blood but doesn't know if it's from his bit tongue or from Cagney. He keeps biting until he can taste flesh through the guy's pants.

Cagney lets out a roar and shakes Marcus around, finally flings him off. Cagney then jumps up to open the service hatch. He jumps up again and heaves himself out of the elevator car. Whips out a gun and starts firing from above.

Five shots nearly hit Marcus who's scrambling on his belly for a gun. With all his strength, he grabs one of the guns and gets to his feet, then jumps up for the service hatch as well. He heaves himself out of the elevator as it continues to climb to the penthouse.

A bullet zings past him as he gets his footing. Then Cagney is upon him, a crazed beast, babbling in tongues, his face red enough to believe that steam should be spewing from his ears.

"I'll    kill    ya,    I'll    kill    ya,    I'll    kill yaaaaaaaaaaaaaaaaaaaa."

Cagney knocks the gun out of Marcus's hand and pries open Marcus's jaw. He sticks his gun into Marcus's mouth, forcing him to choke on it.

"Eat a bullet, eat a bullet, eat a bullet."

Cagney fires, but no bullets come out. The five

holes he made in the elevator plus the most recent shot had emptied the gun.

Marcus grabs at Cagney's face, trying to rip off the mask so he can cause actual harm. But the mask won't budge. He's never seen one so real before.

"What the hell...?"

"That's my real face, asshole. Sliced the old one up and made a new me. That's what Gable's planning to do to every operative now."

Marcus touches the guy's skin. It feels as real as if Cagney was born with it. He thinks of how destroyed someone must be to permanently want a new face. But he knows Cagney's story, so he's not surprised. As a little kid, Cagney's pop beat him to a pulp for sneezing, while his mother loved him unconditionally. Then a purse snatching gone awry left his mother dead in an alleyway while Cagney witnessed the whole thing. His pop wanted nothing to do with him, handing him over to an orphanage full of bullies that liked to beat the new kids to a pulp nightly. He took to boxing as a defense. Boxing soon became his lifeblood. As a teen he found a manager, his career getting lightning hot until his face got pulverized during a mismatched fight, the opponent turning him into a Picasso portrait. He lost all his endorsements, his girl too, turned to petty crime and heroin, in and out of jail. Got swooped up by the Desire Card after owing money to a monster of a crime boss named O' Sullivan who Gable wanted out of the picture as well. O' Sullivan had been trying to pilfer some of Gable's operatives. The crime boss should have known that nothing could be a faster way to die. Gable knew O' Sullivan owned a butcher shop in the Bronx as a front so on Cagney's first day at the

Card, Gable had him sneak into the back of the shop after it closed one night and wait for O' Sullivan with a cleaver in his hand. Told him to bring back one of O' Sullivan's fingers as proof, an act of vengeance Gable liked to repeat again and again. Soon after the O' Sullivan kill, Cagney rose to the rank of operative status faster than anyone else at the Card in twenty years, the fastest since Gable's first protégée Errol Flynn in the late 1970s. Cagney soon became a station agent, known as #2 around the main office. Cagney often liked to tell all the trainees his origin story, as if his tale of rebirth would best everyone else's for the rest of time.

Because of all of this, Cagney's new face would be his greatest pride. So Marcus digs in his nails into Cagney's cheeks, scratches the real skin away so Cagney would have wounds that could never heal.

Cagney shrieks, his horrific screech echoing through the elevator shaft.

Marcus jams his knee into the guy's crotch. He does it again to make sure he hits a testicle this time.

Cagney drops to the roof of the elevator, his hands cupped over his balls.

"You've risked exposing us, Dean," he shouts, angry spit flying from his lips. "It's too dangerous for you or anyone you know to stay alive."

"But somehow I manage to keep ticking."

"Not for long," Cagney says, with a devil's smile. "Have fun getting crushed."

Cagney rolls over and flings himself down the service hatch, thudding to the bottom of the elevator.

Marcus turns around as the ceiling accelerates towards him at an alarming rate. He leaps for the service hatch, falling through and landing on his face just as the elevator stops at the Penthouse floor.

He sees Cagney rushing outside. He feels for the other gun he had dropped earlier, finally grabs it and struggles to his feet. A glance in the elevator's mirror reveals a man who looks like he's been tortured: an eye that has closed over, a busted lip, broken nose, and most likely a broken jaw too. He lurches into a hallway, only one door at the end. His vision is poor, but he can make out the silhouettes of three people in the room.

He shakes his head back and forth as one of the silhouettes comes into focus.

It's Cagney, wiping the blood off his ugly mug with a handkerchief.

Marcus shakes his head again until he can recognize another silhouette.

Annie with a gun pointed in her back.

He shakes his head one last time until the final silhouette is revealed.

Gable with his finger on the trigger.

## 47

THE REALITY OF THE SITUATION TAKES A MOMENT for Marcus to absorb. Not everyone will make it out of this room alive; that is a guarantee. He's got his gun aimed at Gable, Gable's pointing his at Annie, and Cagney's got Marcus in his sights. Marcus knows he's capable of taking out all three, but he needs some questions answered first.

Annie's hysterical, her face full of tears, out of breath.

"Oh, J.D., thank God," she cries. Hard to tell if it's a performance, but that can't be his concern now. Marcus's main focus must be Gable.

"James Dean," Clark Gable says, his robotic tone more of a soothing purr. "What a ride it has been, no?"

"Whatever happens here, I will put a bullet in you," Marcus says. "I will end the Card."

Gable looks over at Cagney and they share in a laugh.

"Impossible, the Card can never end. We are too engrained in the fabric of society. We are what the who's-who whisper about. We are that status symbol that everyone aspires to reach. Some of our most special clients secretly rule the world. You have been with us for seven years now, Dean, you know of our global reach."

"I'm not James Dean. That isn't my name. Just like he isn't Cagney and you are not Gable."

Again, Gable turns to Cagney to share in a laugh.

"You are absolutely right," Gable says. "I know exactly who I am, and I keep this double life very separate. Better than you were able to."

"Is that why your son is in Macau right now?"

Gable tilts his head slightly. It's the first time Marcus has ever seen the Boss threatened. The flash of emotion only lasts for a millisecond before it gets switched off.

"So you found my little secret here," Gable chuckles.

"Room 6129 at the Cotai Strip Casino and Hotel."

"Is this supposed to unnerve me, Dean? Throw me off my game?"

"I imagine that the maid will be more affected when she goes to clean his room."

The look between Gable and Cagney is more serious now, no laughter anymore.

"Chipper invited me right up," Marcus says. "Insisted on being tied to the bed and squealed like a pig when I choked him."

Gable doesn't move, impossible to tell how he's reacting.

"Is Chip dead?" Gable finally asks, the robotic pitch more pronounced than before.

"Maybe he's dead, maybe he's not. I guess you'll have to just wait and see."

Gable disengages the safety on the gun, shoves it into Annie's cheek.

"Do you love this woman?" Gable asks.

There's an energy surrounding Gable that wasn't there before, almost supernatural in its aura, a veil of pure evil. Marcus can feel it entering the room, sucking up all the life, waiting for blood to be shed.

"You do love her, Dean, I can tell. I have loved many in my long life and I know that look, I wear it every day. You've thought about her a lot over the years. On missions where she was all the comfort you had. You often dreamed of that week you spent together before Iraq gobbled you up. And then these past few days, the time apart had intensified every touch. She was on fire, wasn't she, Dean? You just couldn't let go of her charm."

"Has Annie been working for you all along?" he asks. "Was she an operative right under my nose? A plan B in case I ever decided to leave your sick cult and you needed to hunt me down?"

Gable manages to laugh again, but it's not as hardy as the other ones.

"Do you think I've been setting up chess moves eight years in advance just to fuck with you? Do you think you are so *goddamn* important that I would take all that fucking time out of my busy schedule to play some cocksucking game with you? You are nobody. You may have a sharp shot, but I have an army."

"An army I've dwindled down."

"An army you have barely dented," Gable shouts, but his anger tells Marcus that the Card has been damaged. Losing six operatives, seven in total including himself, wouldn't be that easy to replace.

"So to answer your question, no, your little bitch isn't an operative. And we didn't even force her to come to Macau. When Jimmy Stewart came to your house, she sold you out in a heartbeat, said she'd let us use her as bait for ten grand up front and ten more once we got you. Turns out the coke job you guys did barely covered her debts. Shit she's owed to some dumb fucking gangster for years."

"J.D., he's lying, they said they were gonna kill my family."

"She really should win an Oscar," Gable says. "She was gonna con you to keep all the money from her boyfriend's job and she's conning you again by being the one to bring you to me."

Gable takes her face in his hand.

"And you did so well," he says to her, nose to nose. "And you have such a rough beauty about you. You have had a lot of pain in your life, I see it all over you."

He sticks the gun into her temple.

"J.D, oh my God, J.D.!"

"Did you fucking kill my son?" Gable screams at Marcus.

"No, no I didn't–"

"Did you fucking kill my son, you despicable excuse for a human?"

"Don't shoot her," Marcus pleads. "Your son...he's still alive. He's tied up in his room, he's fine...I just needed him to get to you."

"J.D., I swear I wasn't conning you," Annie wails. She's cried so much she has no tears left, the words spewing from her mouth in dry heaves.

Marcus and her lock eyes. He finds himself diving inside her pupils, one last shot to see if she's true and real.

"You and me in paradise, J.D....that's all I ever wanted," Annie says. "Meetin' on that island...where a volcano erupted and made a white sand beach...made it beautiful again."

"Matagi Island," he whispers.

"Matagi Island," she mouths back to him.

"Do you promise that you didn't kill my son?" Gable asks, softer this time, as if he's ready to relent, to put the gun down and call it a truce, walk their separate ways, never speak again.

"I promise...your son is still alive. I wouldn't do that. I'm not that far gone yet."

"Too bad I am," Gable says, firing his gun. The bullet shoots through Annie's brain, her mouth frozen in the shape of a blown kiss. She collapses to the floor, immediately surrounded by a pool of blood.

Marcus is upon her instantly, scooping her up, sobbing into her cheek, squeezing her body and praying for a sign of life. Then reality sets in, the immediacy of both Gable and Cagney drawing their guns.

While still holding onto Annie, Marcus quickly gets off a shot and hits Cagney in the leg. Cagney falls back, his gun firing into the ceiling.

Marcus expects Gable to shoot, but Gable runs over to a bookcase and removes a book. The bookcase opens to a secret passage.

"Car," Gable yells at Cagney, before he disappears into the secret passage.

Marcus spins around to fire at Cagney again, but Cagney is already out the door into the hallway.

The room is eerily silent now. He lets Annie slip from his arms. He closes her eyes and leaves a final kiss, one without any anger for what she may have done, a kiss for that week they spent together so long ago, a kiss that apologizes for charging back into her life. For making a girl like her have to decide whether or not to turn on him when her own life was already in danger and some cash could mean a fresh start.

"You and me in paradise?" he says. "That's a joke if I ever heard one."

As he stands, he's only filled with rage. It builds and builds until it takes over, changes a man. He runs inside the secret passage with one final goal: The Boss's head punted from this casino into the clouds.

But first Gable needs to know that while his son has been spared, the rest of Gable's family might not be so lucky now.

## 48

THE SECRET PASSAGE IN THE BOOKSHELF LEADS TO A room of mirrors and a winding staircase. At the top Marcus can vaguely see the lights of Macau beaming down until the door to the roof is shut. As he runs up the stairs, he sees a million reflections of himself. He tries not to look at any of them. He no longer knows who he is anymore and what he's capable of doing.

At the top of the twisting staircase is a lone door. He barrels through it and steps out to a large terrace at the tip-top of the casino. Macau's skyline flashes its glitz, a demented futuristic world where the kings are whoever's the best con man. He's crying, he's bleeding, he's numb, he's hungry, he's thirsty, he's tired, he's lived too many lives in this short one; he's done. There's nothing left in him but the gun in his hand and a promise to complete the mission, even if death is the reward.

Gable is over by the ledge putting on a backpack.

Marcus raises his gun as Gable does the same.

"You didn't have to kill her," Marcus says, surprised

at what comes out of his mouth, running on only instinct now.

"Even after what I told you about her, Dean?" Gable says, calm as ever, as if a showdown like this happens every day. "Annie was an opportunist, but maybe that doesn't bother you because you're an opportunist too. You have no loyalty, you ride along from selfish whim to selfish whim."

"She didn't have to die."

"Or maybe part of you believes that Annie was telling the truth. Is that what it is? Your infatuation with her makes you supersede all common logic. But you know what? Maybe I did make it all up. Maybe I had Jimmy Stewart bind her and ship her like fucking cargo on a private plane here. Maybe I showed her parents' cheap wedding rings to prove that I meant business. Maybe I said that if she didn't help me get you, I'd gut her like a fish and toss her body in the Pearl River."

Marcus's finger flirts with the trigger, knowing that Gable would get a shot off as well, deciding if he's ready for this moment to be his last.

"You, my friend, will never know if sweet Annie was really sour. If she deserved to die."

"Either way she didn't deserve to die."

"You always liked to think of yourself as so noble. The Iraqi veteran who lost an eye and never got the chance to shine on the battlefield. Such a tragic tale. The tiny orphan raised by a kooky old man until little Dean had to learn to raise himself."

"Yeah, you collect people like us, Gable. You like them desperate, don't you?"

"My operatives come from many walks of life. They are not all white trash travesties like yourself. But yes, I do look for a singular trait and you fit that profile to a T."

"Because I was damaged?"

"Because you are immoral. Because you've done things so hideous in your past. That woman and her baby in Iraq. The truly defining moment of your life. After that, all you could see ahead of you was a lifetime of addictions and an early grave; but then you found salvation in my arms. You honed your skills, even with your infliction. I was proud to call you a son, for all my operatives are my children, my family. Do you know what it does to me when I lose one? It is like taking a limb, that is our bond."

"You don't give a shit about any of us. You'll knock us off the minute we don't serve a purpose–"

"That is not true, I only terminate an operative when they become a threat to the Card."

"You didn't have to hunt me. You could have just let me go and none of them would've died—Bogart, Rita, the international operatives, Jimmy Stewart...Annie..."

"You posed a risk of exposing everything–"

"But I never would've told anyone! I would have disappeared and did the rest of my time on this Earth in silence and never would've been a threat."

"That's naïve, Dean. People talk, they say things, they get wasted and open up, they fall in love and open up. I can't spend my life worrying that you might slip one day. I'd rather not have to think about you at all."

"Do you think about any of the tombstones you've been responsible for? The lives you've destroyed?"

"The lives I've destroyed are far less than the ones I have made even greater."

"I'm sure you tell yourself that to help you go to

sleep each night. I know just what that is like. Every time I try to dream it only turns into nightmares."

"Well, I don't sleep, Jimmy Dean. Sleep is for mortals."

"Right, the devil doesn't need to nap."

"Is that what you think of me? That I am the devil? What a compliment."

"Yeah, you're the fucking devil, and the devil's gonna die today."

Gable starts to chuckle until it turns into the insane laugh of someone possessed.

"So you shoot me and vengeance is served for your ol' Kentucky gal? Or for Hasan Bouchtat, or for that girl in the alleyway, or for the first time I showed you who you truly were, Dean?"

"No, you made me into this killer."

"Killers aren't made, they are born. I may have shaped you, I may have polished you, but I did not make you. You were born with a metal heart."

"The things you had me do," Marcus says, fighting not to breakdown, keeping his hand steady, keeping Gable in his sight.

"I told you from your first day at the Card that nothing was outside our ethical boundaries. You knew exactly who we were from the start, just like I knew exactly who you were. You closed that one eye of yours and convinced yourself that I was your future because you were a doped-up ex-grunt with a house in foreclosure and I was the only option you had. But the truth is you *loooooooved* it. The thrill of a gun in your hand again, the orgasm of a perfect shot. You're a sniper. It's in your blood. It's all you'll ever be."

"If that's the case then you don't stand a chance right now."

"Sorry to be a spoilsport, but I'm wearing a bullet-proof vest."

"The gun is aimed right between your eyes."

"The mask is bulletproof too. You can't kill me, Dean, because I won't die. At the end, it'll just be me and the cockroaches. That is how long I will endure. And you will always be looking over your shoulder. Even if you survive this standoff today, it won't matter because I am everywhere: watching, waiting, and then deciding when to pounce. And when I do, I go for the jugular. I'll make you struggle. I'll gather all your worst fears and make sure every one of them happens. I'll drag out your death until you're begging me, pleading, and then I'll leave you alive for the bugs to have their way with you...while I watch it all, cigar in hand."

Marcus reaches into his pocket and pulls out the photograph of Gable's family.

"I know exactly what your real family looks like, Gable. If I survive today, I'll find them. Your wife, your daughter? I'll scar them both so bad that the only place they'll fit in is as one your operatives."

Gable has become completely silent, no telling how he's reacting behind the mask.

"Or what about your grandchildren? The little girl is mighty cute. I think I can even read the name of the school on her uniform. Chapin School for Girls, is it? Wouldn't it be a shame if I was there to pick her up one day?"

"You motherfucking–"

Gable fires the gun, hitting Marcus in the shoulder.

Marcus gets off a shot as well, striking Gable right between the eyes, the bullet bouncing off.

"See?" Gable growls. "I said you were a killer all along."

Marcus fires another shot hitting Gable in the chest. The bullet causes Gable to stumble back. Marcus fires again and again, forcing Gable towards the ledge until a final shot sends him twisting over.

As Gable plummets to the street below, the mask flies off of his face.

Marcus runs to the ledge, desperate to see the face behind the mask, but Gable has fallen too far already. He's nothing more than a black dot spiraling down into the abyss.

———

After taking the elevator, Marcus bursts out of the Excelsior Casino, his one eye scanning for a sign of Gable's exploded body. All he sees is an abandoned parachute. Next to it is the Clark Gable mask.

"No," he shouts, kicking at the parachute. "No, no, no!"

From inside him erupts a terrifying scream, loud enough to feel like the Earth is shaking. He picks up the Gable mask, his heart pounding.

"You will always be looking over your shoulder," he hears, and turns around in fright.

"Who said that?"

The adjacent street is full of people. He scans their faces frantically. Any one of them could be Gable.

But then his eye zeroes in on a man weaving

through the crowd. The man is covering his face with his hand.

Marcus raises his gun, trying to line up the shot. There are too many people on the street to be certain he'll hit Gable, but he's willing to take that chance. He's that far gone now.

As he goes to pull the trigger, a car swerves past him and careens towards the crowded street. He sees that Cagney's at the wheel, the guy's cheeks still bleeding from when Marcus dug in with his fingernails.

The car speeds into the crowd as the passenger side door opens. The man covering his face jumps inside.

Marcus pulls the trigger, the bullet hitting the car but it doesn't stop. Then the car turns on a main road and is lost in Macau's chaotic traffic.

Marcus sinks to his knees. The Clark Gable mask slips from his hand.

He watches the mask spin around and around until it finally slows down and comes to a dead stop.

# EPILOGUE

MARCUS STANDS ACROSS THE STREET FROM THE Chapin school for girls. He's dressed entirely in black, a part of the shadows. New York's afternoon light is waning; the street crowded enough for him to blend in. He has been meticulously planning this since he returned from Macau. He just needed to wait for daylight-saving time to begin so it could get dark an hour earlier.

In his hand is a copy of *The Call of the Wild*, a passage underlined.

> *"He was a killer, a thing that preyed, living on the things that lived, unaided, alone, by virtue of his own strength and prowess, surviving triumphantly in a hostile environment where only the strong survive."*

He reads it again and again and again, even saying it out loud so the gods might hear, so they might understand.

The school bell rings.

He sticks *The Call of the Wild* back in his pocket. This causes his shoulder to hurt, the sensation like being burned repeatedly with a cigarette. He fixes the sling around his shoulder and gives the muscle a good rub. Then he takes out the photo of Gable's family and stares at the granddaughter posing in her school uniform.

The front door to the school opens and a flood of little girls in uniforms all pile out.

After a minute, he spies the girl in the picture. Prim and poised, walking on her toes, no more than nine years old.

He stuffs the photo in his pocket. Follows her.

Along the gridlocked streets, he makes sure to stay at least three people back. Avenue after avenue he keeps her tiny head in his sights.

Soon she enters Central Park, walking from the Eastside to the West. She turns onto the Ramble, a dizzying maze of woodland trails. He has seen her take this route before. It is ideal since no one's around.

He stays right behind her but at enough of a distance so she can't tell. She's caught up in an ever-important text message. This is the first time he's seen that she has her own phone, which is key since Gable's number is probably in her contacts.

They wind down the Ramble, the sunset flickering through the overhead trees.

Creeping closer, he steps on a branch by accident causing it to snap.

The little girl spins around, but he hides behind a weeping willow. He watches her like always, imagining a chloroform-soaked rag covering her mouth as she collapses in his arms, her snores so delicate. Then he'd pick her up and carry her out of the park, just as if she's his baby girl who's fallen asleep on his shoulder. The one possible thing in Gable's world that might give Marcus some leverage, allow him a chance at a trade for freedom.

The last bit of sunset light is still trickling through the leaves, as she looks closer into the tree. But for now, he is still, patient as ever, until he will strike with his final play in an attempt to end this maddening game.

**A DEVILISHLY DARK THRILLER THAT EXPLORES HOW FAR A MAN WILL GO TO SURVIVE WHEN MONEY ISN'T ALWAYS ENOUGH TO GET EVERYTHING HE DESIRES.**

*Any wish fulfilled for the right price.* That's the promise the organization behind The Desire Card gives to its elite clients. But sometimes the price is more menacing than anyone ever imagined.

Harrison Stockton has lived an adult life of privilege and excess. A high-powered job on Wall Street fuels his fondness for alcohol and pills at the expense of a family he has no time for. Quite suddenly, all of his luxuries come to a crashing halt when he loses his job and—at the same time—discovers he has just months left to live.

Desperate, and with seemingly nowhere else left to turn, Harrison activates his Desire Card. What follows is a gritty and gripping quest that takes him from New York City to the slums of Mumbai, where he's forced to take chances and make decisions he hoped to never face. And when his moral descent threatens his wife and children, Harrison must decide whether to save himself at any cost...or do what's right and break his bargain with The Desire Card.

A taut and fast-paced thriller, *All Sins Fulfilled* follows those indebted to this sinister organization—where the ultimate price is the cost of one's soul.

*"I couldn't look away for a moment from Harrison Stockton's thrilling train wreck of a life. Jeer at him, cheer for him, and maybe—just*

*maybe—fall in love with him a little. Lee Matthew Goldberg has created a Bonfire of the Vanities for a new generation, and served it up with style, wit, and empathy. I guarantee you'll want to devour The Desire Card series in one glorious, heart-pounding sitting."* —**Laura Benedict, Edgar nominated author of** *The Stranger Inside*

*AVAILABLE JULY 2022*

# ABOUT THE AUTHOR

**Lee Matthew Goldberg** is the author of eight novels including *The Ancestor* and *The Mentor* and the YA series *Runaway Train*. His books are in various stages of development for film and TV off of his original scripts. He has been published in multiple languages and nominated for the Prix du Polar. *Stalker Stalked* will be out in Fall '21. After graduating with an MFA from the New School, his writing has also appeared as a contributor in *Pipeline Artists*, *LitHub*, *The Los Angeles Review of Books*, *The Millions*, *Vol. 1 Brooklyn*, *LitReactor*, *The Big Idea*, *Monkeybicycle*, *Fiction Writers Review*, *Cagibi*, *Necessary Fiction*, *Hypertext*, *If My Book*, *Past Ten*, the anthology *Dirty Boulevard*, *The Montreal Review*, *The Adirondack Review*, *The New Plains Review*, *Maudlin House*, *Underwood Press*, and others. His pilots and screenplays have been finalists in *Script Pipeline*, *Book Pipeline*, *Stage 32*, *We Screenplay*, the *New York Screenplay*, *Screencraft*, and the *Hollywood Screenplay* contests. He is the co-curator of *The Guerrilla Lit Reading Series* and lives in New York City. Follow him at LeeMatthewGoldberg.com.

Made in the USA
Monee, IL
23 August 2022

12330001R00144